Jennie Taylor Wandle

The art of modern lace-making

Jennie Taylor Wandle

The art of modern lace-making

ISBN/EAN: 9783741190131

Manufactured in Europe, USA, Canada, Australia, Japa

Cover: Foto ©Andreas Hilbeck / pixelio.de

Manufactured and distributed by brebook publishing software
(www.brebook.com)

Jennie Taylor Wandle

The art of modern lace-making

THE ART

OF

MODERN LACE-MAKING

PRICE:

FIFTY CENTS OR TWO SHILLINGS.

PUBLISHED BY

THE BUTTERICK PUBLISHING CO. (LIMITED).

LONDON AND NEW YORK,

AND PRINTED AT THEIR PRINTING WORKS IN NEW YORK.

1896.

INTRODUCTION.

OWING to the growing popularity of the fascinating art of Modern Lace-Making and the appeals of our readers to place it within their reach, we have revised and greatly enlarged our first book upon the subject. In making a perfect instructor and a reliable exponent of the favorite varieties of lace, we have spared neither time nor expense, and are most happy to offer to our patrons what a celebrated maker of Modern Lace, with whose assistance and under whose direction the book was prepared, has pronounced "the finest book upon lace-making to be found upon either continent."

The illustrations, in the main, are direct reproductions from genuine, hand-made Modern Laces, such as any lady may make who masters the instructions found upon the pages of this book. The beauty of Modern Laces is beyond question, their durability all that can be desired, and their textures varied from an extreme delicacy to a sumptuous opposite.

Except to introduce some of the stitches employed in the needle or pillow laces, we have not taken up either of these varieties of old laces for reasons which will be perfectly apparent to the reader of the pages devoted to "Ancient and Modern Methods." The requirements of the present day, with the majority, are for handsome laces of a comparatively inexpensive quality; laces that can be easily made, and at the same time are effective. Modern point, Honiton, Point de Bruges, Royal Battenburg, Ideal Honiton, etc., meet the requirements named, and we therefore deal with them alone in offering this book. In introducing the art of Modern Lace-Making into the realms of our readers, we feel all the pleasure we are sure we thus convey.

THE BUTTERICK PUBLISHING CO. (Limited).

CONTENTS.

Royal Battenburg Tea-Cloth Awarded First Prize at World's Fair. (See page 36.)

The Art of Lace-Making.

ANCIENT AND MODERN METHODS.

HE art of making lace in one form or another has existed from the earliest ages. There are Scriptural references to various web-like fabrics, which were of rude construction, no doubt, but whose general characteristics were identical with those productions of modern skill which have for centuries been known as lace. Homer and other ancient writers constantly mention networks of fanciful embroidered materials; gold thread-work was known to the Romans; and as Egyptian robes of state are depicted upon the tombs of the earlier dynasties as being fashioned from a looped network or crochet, it is probable that the Israelites learned the art from the Egyptians. Museums contain specimens of lace dating back to periods that to us of the present day seem mere dreams of reigns and eras, and history includes a scattered literature of lace which proves that the art must have been practised almost from the beginning.

Up to the Sixteenth Century, however, open-work embroidery was the favorite decoration, and from it the tangible origin of lace seems derived. During the Renaissance period the first book of embroidery patterns and lace-work appeared. The earliest volume bearing a date was printed at Cologne in 1527; and it was during the reign of Richard III. of England that the word lace was first used in the description of the royal wardrobe.

At first the best known laces were those of Venice, Milan and Genoa. The Italians claim the invention of point or needle-made lace; but the Venetian point is now a product of the past, and England and France supply most of the fine laces of the present time.

Lace-makers in the various European countries are trained to the work from childhood; but it is said of the makers of Honiton lace, the fabric of which Queen Victoria's wedding gown was made, that they are rapidly decreasing in numbers, so that there are few persons now living who understand the construction of this exquisite "pillow" lace. The costly point and Honiton and the dainty Mechlin and Valenciennes of by-gone days can only be produced by trained lace-workers, whose skilful fingers weave bobbins of cobweb-like thread to and fro over the "pillow" necessary to antique methods; and for this reason fine lace-making is practically beyond the skill of the amateur. Besides, some of the threads in the very filmy laces are so fine that they cannot be successfully manipulated except in a moist atmosphere, such as that of Great Britain; and even there some of the more exquisite specimens must perforce be made in underground rooms, since it is only there that the proper degree of moisture can be obtained. In dry climates these gossamer-like threads roughen and break at almost the slightest touch.

Referring to the known origin of some of the earlier laces, a writer upon the subject says:

"They say it was a woman, Barbara Uttmann, who invented pillow lace in the Sixteenth Century. Women have ever been patrons of lace-making. Victoria has kept the Honiton laces in fashion, and it was the Duchess of Argyle who introduced lace-making into Scotland. The Countess of Erne and Lady Denny and Lady Bingham began it in Ireland, and Lady De Vere gave her own Brussels point for patterns when the first Irish point was made at Currah. It was Elizabeth of Denmark who introduced lace-making in that country, and the Archduchess Sophia who started lace schools in Bohemia. 'Now, at least, I can have laces,' said Anne of Austria, when Louis XIII, her husband died, and her court was famous for its cleanliness and its Spanish point. Colbert had three women as coadjutors when he started lace-making in France. It was because Josephine loved point d'Alençon that Napoleon revived it. Eugenie spent $5,000 for a single dress flounce, and had $1,000,000 in fine laces."

Victoria's favorite, Honiton, is not considered a particularly beautiful lace, although its weaving is so tedious and difficult. "Real Honiton laces," says an authority, "are made up of bits and bits fashioned by many different women in their own little cottages —here a leaf, there a flower, slowly woven through the long, weary days, only to be united afterward in the precious web by other workers who never saw its beginning. There is a pretty lesson in the thought that to the perfection of each of these little pieces the beauty of the whole is due—that the rose or leaf some humble peasant woman wrought carefully, helps to make the fabric worthy the adorning of a queen or the devotion of an altar, even as the sweetness and patient perfection in any life makes all living more worthy and noble. A single flower upon which taste and fancy were lavished, and which sustained and deft labor brought to perfection, represents the lives of many diligent women workers.

It has become so the fashion to worship all things ancient that most lovers of fine lace would prefer to have it a century old; and yet there never was a time when laces were more beautiful, more artistic and more unique in design than just at the present day; for modern laces preserve the best features of the laces that have gone before them, and have added so many new inspirations that except for the sentiment, the romance or the history connecting this scrap with a title, that with a famous beauty, and another with some cathedral's sacred treasure, the palm would certainly be given to the gauze-like production of the poor flax thread spinner of the present day."

Not all the people know the difference between point lace which is made with the needle, and pillow lace which is made with the bobbins—but much of the beautiful point lace of the present day is made with the needle, and its beauty stands a favorable comparison with the more costly pillow lace.

Strictly Modern Lace-Making is a result of American ingenuity, and it has so simple a basis and is so easy to learn that any woman of average skill may, with little difficulty, produce by its different processes, laces that are really magnificent and quite as substantial and useful as they are exquisitely beautiful. In America Modern Lace-Making has been developed to a high degree of perfection by the skill of Miss Sara Hadley, in whose designing rooms at No. 923 Broadway, New York, may be seen specimens of modern laces of every variety, from dainty needle-point to a very elaborate kind known as the Royal Battenburg. This English name for an American production was selected in honor of the Battenburg nuptials, which occurred about the time the lace was introduced.

Materials Used in Modern Lace-Making.

THE requirements of Modern Lace-Making are few. The products are classed as Honiton, Point, Needle-Point, Duchess, Princess, Royal Battenburg or Old English Point, Point de Bruges, Limoges, and Ideal Honiton; but all are made with various braids arranged in different patterns and connected by numerous kinds of stitches, many different stitches often appearing in one variety of lace. Many varieties of Modern Lace are developed by combining one or more of the kinds specified above.

The materials required are neither numerous nor expensive. The following is a complete list: Tracing cloth, leather or *toile cirée*, lace braids of various kinds, linen thread of proper textures or sizes, two or three sizes of needles, a good thimble and a pair of fine sharp scissors.

For each kind of lace there is a special sort of braid in various patterns, as will be seen by referring to pages 12, 13, 14 and 15; and the selection of the thread depends entirely upon the variety and quality of lace to be made. This selection should be left to the decision of the teacher or the skilled maker of laces, as she knows from experience the proper combinations of materials. Thus, in making Honiton and point lace, thread in twelve different degrees of fineness is used; and as the braids also vary in size, the thread must always be adapted to the braid. For Battenburg lace the thread is in eight sizes, the finest being used only for "whipping curves" or drawing edges into the outlines required. The other laces all have their special threads which will be designated by any lace maker of whom inquiries are made.

The "Ideal Honiton" is a new lace made with fancy Honiton braid and wash-silk floss in dainty colors, and is exquisite for doileys, mats, table and bureau scarfs and center-pieces. The design is traced on fine linen lawn, the braid is then basted on, and fastened down with short and long button-hole-stitches and a pointed edge of the same is added, after which the material is cut away from the scollops and from under the braid. Any of the numerous illustrations of Ideal Honiton seen on the following pages will perfectly disclose the method of making.

Designs sold by lace-makers are usually drawn upon tracing cloth, as this is flexible and much more agreeable to work upon than any other material. The tracing cloth, when the braid is arranged, is basted to a foundation of leather or *toile cirée*; or smooth wrapping-paper may be basted under the design and will furnish all the support that is necessary, while being lighter than the *toile cirée*.

It must be remembered that the work, except in Ideal Honiton lace, is really wrong side out while in progress, so that it will not show its true beauty until finished and removed from the foundation or pattern. According to the braid and thread selected, these laces may be made of fairy-like fineness or of massive elegance—general results being dainty enough for the gown of a bride or sumptuous enough for the adornment of an altar.

Lace-making establishments will furnish designs of any width or shape desired, and will also originate designs for special articles for which there are only occasional calls. Regular edging designs are ordinarily made in four widths—from quite narrow to very wide; and not infrequently a handkerchief design is enlarged sufficiently to form a square for a table or a fancy stand.

In filling in the spaces of any design or pattern, the worker may choose the stitches that please her best, if she does not like those accompanying the design that she has selected or that has been sent her. She will find upon these pages over a hundred specimens of stitches which are in a department by themselves; and these, with the many designs of laces also given, should supply her with all the material and instruction necessary to aid her in the production of any of the varieties of Modern Lace.

Fancy Braids, Cords, Floral Ornaments, Rings and Buttons Used in Making Modern Lace.

In making modern lace, the various kinds require appropriate braids. There are several classes of these braids—those for Battenburg and Bruges laces, those for Honiton, Point, Duchess or Princess; and those for the newest kind of lace, which is called "Ideal Honiton." Each class of braids contains many designs and widths, and a large number of them, together with various cords, buttons and rings also used are illustrated on the following pages.

BRAIDS AND CORDS.

The braids, cords, rings and buttons illustrated upon the following pages are all used in Modern Lace-Making. They are all made of pure linen thread, and according to the fancy, the lace including them may be heavy or light. Royal Battenburg lace, as originated, was heavy—in some cases massive; but at present many lighter varieties are made, as will be sur-mised upon an inspection of the braids for its manufacture which are represented on the pages mentioned. These and all the other braids are given in their actual width. The num-bers opposite the specimens are simply for convenience in ordering, if the order is sent to the lady whose name is mentioned below and also in another part of the book; but in ordering from other lace makers or manufacturers of braids these numbers will be of little use, as every lace-maker or manufacturer has his or her own individual identifications for materials. Almost any of the braids, or those very similar, may be found at large fancy stores; but in buying them at such stores be careful to get *linen* braids, as cotton braids do not make pretty lace, neither do they wear or launder well. In ordering these braids from other lace-makers or from fancy stores, it will be necessary to forward the illustration of the kind wanted, as the braids cannot be described with sufficient accuracy to obtain the desired varieties. Some are sold by the yard, some by the dozen yards and others by the piece, according to the position to be occupied in the work.

The Point, Honiton, Duchess and Princess braids are much daintier in texture than the Battenburg braids. Of this class of braids (see Nos. 7, 9 and 10, page 13) are made the plain Honiton and point laces, and the braids for these two laces combined produce the Princess lace—a creation whose beauty fully entitles it to its royal name.

The braids seen at Nos. 11, 12 and 13, page 14, are those which are used in making Ideal Honiton lace, represented in another part of the book. This is one of the prettiest laces made, and as before mentioned is very appropriate for tidies, doileys, squares and bureau scarfs.

The cords seen at No. 2, page 12, are used in making Battenburg laces, and greatly increase the beauty of the work in addition to forming a distinctive species of lace (see page 100). After the ordinary Battenburg is worked with quite thick braid, the cord, in any size desired, is used to follow one edge of the design, as will be seen from the illustrations referred to.

RINGS AND BUTTONS.

The rings and buttons illustrated at No. 2, page 12, are made throughout of linen thread in layers of button-hole stitches worked over a foundation ring of wound thread, and are sold by the dozen or gross by their inventor, Miss Sara Hadley, of 923 Broadway, New York. Intelligent lace-makers can, by an inspection of the designs, and an observance of the hint given in this paragraph, make them for themselves or customers with no difficulty. Buttons arranged as grapes (also see No. 2, page 12), add greatly to the sumptuous effect of a heavy lace, and may be purchased already arranged as illustrated, or they may be arranged by the purchaser of a quantity of them. The latter method is a good plan if spaces are to be filled with clusters which must be of a certain shape. A reference to the frontispiece of this book will disclose a generous use of these buttons and the royal effect they produce.

FLORAL ORNAMENTS.

The ornaments seen on page 15, and the *fleur de lis* at No. 8 upon page 13, are used in Ideal Honiton work, and are also the invention of the clever lace-maker already mentioned. They may be obtained singly, in sets, or by the dozen or gross at her establishment, or may be made by any lace-worker, amateur or professional, as the engravings perfectly show the method necessary to their construction.

These ornaments, applied, may be seen at some of the engravings of Ideal Honiton lace in other parts of the book.

ACTUAL SIZES OF THE LACES AND ARTICLES ILLUSTRATED.

It will be readily understood that it is impossible to give all of the designs and illustrations of the articles represented in this book in their full sizes. For the benefit of those who do not know what the sizes are, we would here say that tumbler or punch glass doileys are usually from three and a half to four inches in diameter ; finger-bowl doileys are from four to five inches across, while other doileys are from six to eight inches in diameter, or of the dimensions required by the dishes or articles they are to rest under or over. Sizes may also be governed entirely by individual taste.

Center-pieces are from twenty-four inches square (or in diameter) to any size necessary to fit the table they are to be used upon.

Edgings and articles of wear are of such widths and dimensions as may be decided by personal taste. Every pattern in the book can be adapted by either a clever amateur, or a professional lace-maker, to any size required. Many of the designs may be used as given.

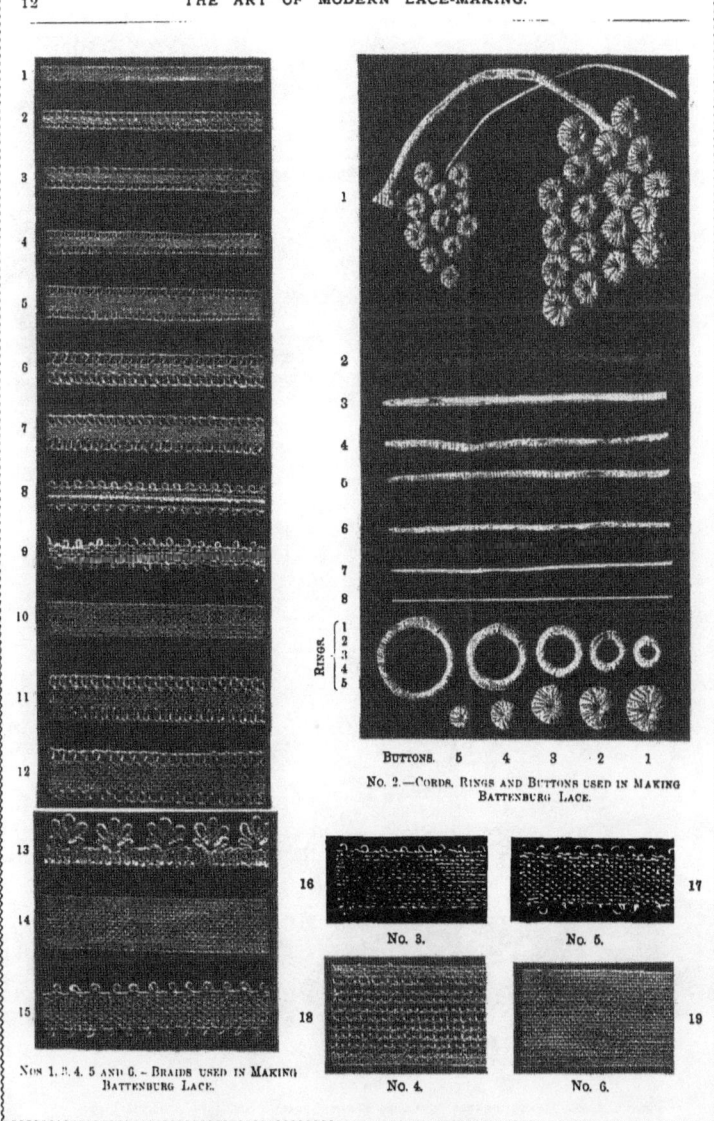

No. 2.—Cords, Rings and Buttons used in Making
Battenburg Lace.

No. 3.

No. 5.

No. 4.

No. 6.

Nos 1, 3, 4, 5 and 6. – Braids used in Making
Battenburg Lace.

No. 8.—Fleur de Lis for Ideal Honiton Lace.

No. 7.

No. 9.

No. 10.

Nos. 7, 9 and 10.—Braids used in Making Honiton, Point, Duchess and Princess Laces.

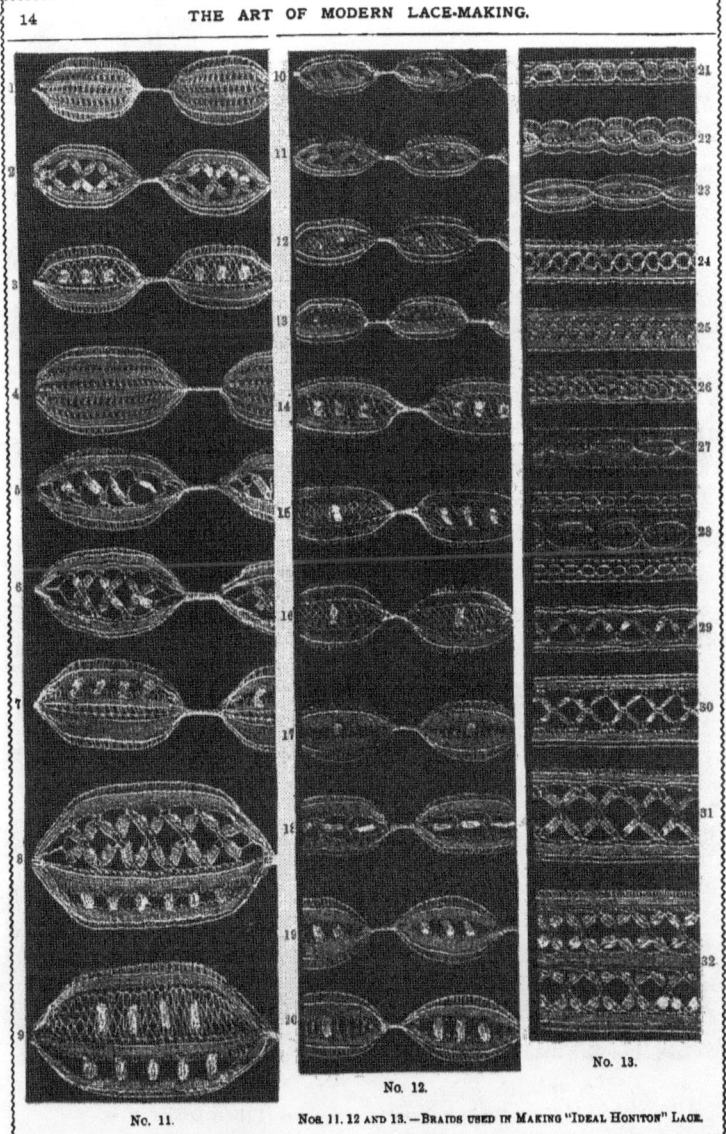

No. 11.

No. 12.

No. 13.

Nos. 11, 12 and 13. — Braids used in Making "Ideal Honiton" Lace.

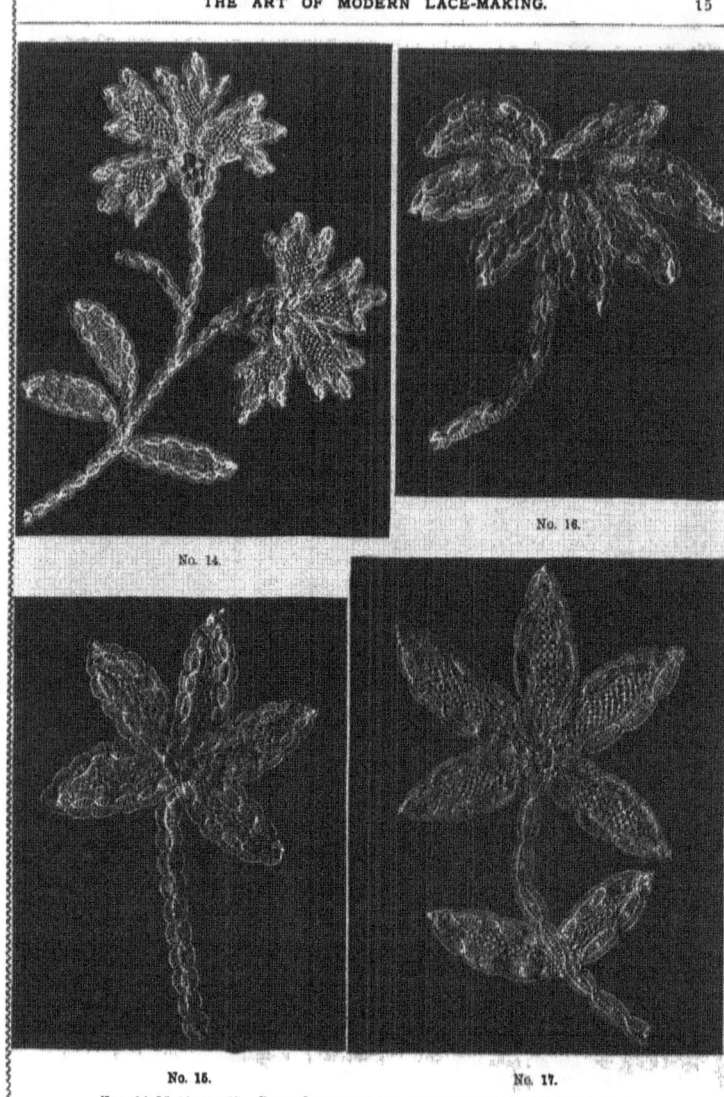

No. 16.

No. 14.

No. 15.

No. 17.

Nos. 14, 15, 16 and 17.—Braid Ornaments used in Making "Ideal Honiton" Work.

STITCHES USED IN MODERN LACE-MAKING.

As in all fancy work which has a set of foundation stitches peculiar to it that may be varied according to the proficiency and ingenuity of the maker, so has Modern Lace a series of primary stitches from which may be evolved many others. A large number of illustrations of stitches, some of which are primary or foundation stitches, while others are combinations, are here presented, with full instructions for making; and the entire series given will make perfectly plain to the student the ease with which she may combine or invent stitches, when those of the design she has to work are not to her liking. The first stitch given is the main foundation stitch.

Nos. 1 TO 5.—POINT DE BRUXELLES OR BRUSSELS POINT.—Among the stitches most used in lace-making is Point de Bruxelles or Brussels Point. It is simply a button-hole stitch worked loosely, and it must be done with regularity, as the beauty of the work depends almost wholly upon the evenness of the stitches. Brussels point is occasionally used as an edge, but is more frequently seen in rows worked back and forth to fill in spaces, or as a ground work. The illustrations clearly represent the method of making this stitch.

Nos. 6, 7, 8, 9 AND 11.—POINT D'ANVERS; NEW POINT DE MALINES. (CORDED BUTTON-HOLE STITCHES.)—No. 6 is a slight variety of the same stitch seen at No. 54 on page 23, under the name of Italian Lace Stitch. In returning, in this pattern, the thread is twisted through the button-hole stitch and is enclosed by the fresh button-hole stitches. This variation is a near approach to the point de Malines. The button-hole stitch is worked between the cording-stitch. Nos. 7 and 9 show leaves in point de Bruxelles and point d'Anvers, and are worked in button-hole stitch, with and without the thread being drawn through; and, in No. 9, filled up as shown, by a cross-stitch. Nos. 8 and 11 give the variations of these patterns, as seen in the large and small patterns of the Antwerp lace, and known to very many ladies as point d'Anvers. No. 8 belongs to the order of button-hole stitches, all the patterns of which being worked by drawing the thread through, may be classed among the Antwerp stitches (point d'Anvers).

It need scarcely be mentioned that the long threads between the spaces are wound round with several stitches.

Nos. 10, 12, 13, 14, 15, 16 AND 17.—POINT DE SORRENTO.—For this stitch, several button-hole stitches are worked close together, and are made in each line as belonging to each other; they are not separated by any stitch. No. 12 represents this stitch as worked for an edge; this, as well as the single stitch (No. 13), makes a very firm edge ornament. No. 10 gives a single-dotted pattern of two button-hole stitches. Nos. 14, 15 and 17 give more varied patterns. No. 16 gives the Sorrento pattern with button-hole stitches over the thread placed across, and from which many other effective stitches may be made.

Nos. 18, 19 AND 20.—POINT TURQUE, OR TURKISH POINT.—This easy and effective stitch is very appropriate for filling either large or small spaces; the thread employed should be varied in thickness according to the size of the space to be filled.

First row (see No. 20).—Work a loop into the braid, bringing the thread from right to left, passing the needle through the twist and through the loop (see engraving); draw up tight and repeat.

Second row.—1 straight thread from right to left.

Third row.—Work the same as first, using the straight thread in place of the braid, and passing the needle through the loop of the previous row, as shown in the illustration. No. 19 represents the stitch on one line, which would make a very pretty outer edge. No. 18 represents the dotted pattern, consisting of one plain and one looped button-hole stitch, which is a pretty variation of No. 19, and might also be worked over threads placed across.

STITCHES USED IN MAKING MODERN LACE.

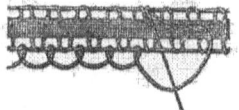

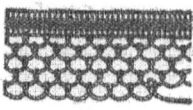

No. 1.—Point de Bruxelles.   No. 2.—Point de Bruxelles (Brussels Point).   No. 3.—Point de Bruxelles Worked in Rows.

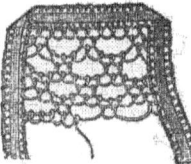
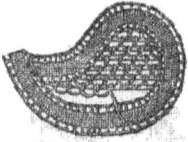
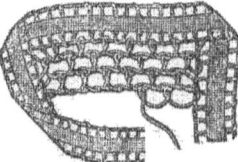

No. 4.—Point de Bruxelles.   No. 5.—Point de Bruxelles.   No. 6.—Corded Button-Hole Stitch.

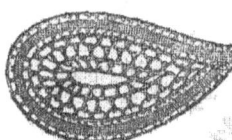
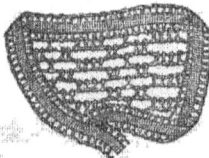

No. 7.—Point d'Anvers (Corded Button-Hole Stitch).   No. 8.—Point d'Anvers (Corded Button-Hole Stitch).   No. 9.—Point d'Anvers (Corded Button-Hole Stitch).

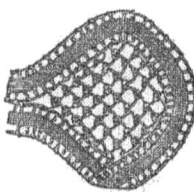

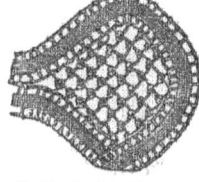
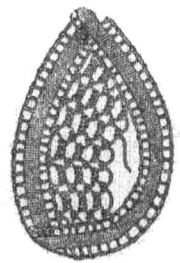

No. 11.—Point d'Anvers (Corded Button-Hole Stitch).

No. 10.—Point de Sorrento.

No. 12.—Point de Sorrento.   No. 13—Point de Sorrento.   No. 14.—Point de Sorrento.

2

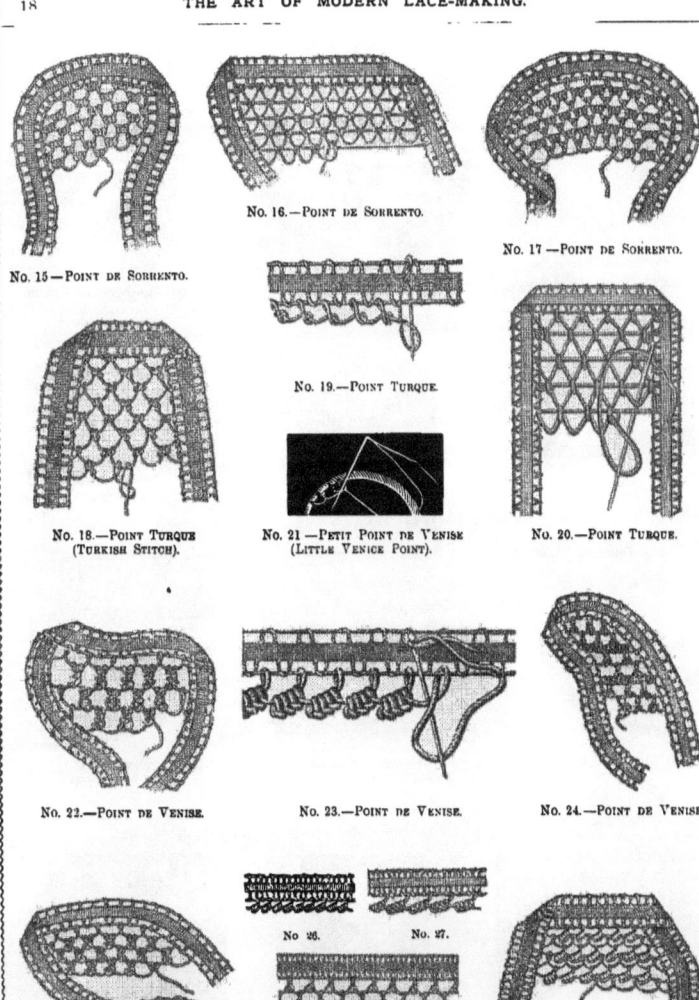

No. 16.—Point de Sorrento.

No. 15—Point de Sorrento.

No. 17.—Point de Sorrento.

No. 19.—Point Turque.

No. 18.—Point Turque (Turkish Stitch).

No. 21.—Petit Point de Venise (Little Venice Point).

No. 20.—Point Turque.

No. 22.—Point de Venise.

No. 23.—Point de Venise.

No. 24.—Point de Venise.

No 26.   No. 27.

No. 28.

No. 25.—Point de Venise.   Nos. 26, 27 and 28.—Point de Venise.   No. 29.—Point de Venise.

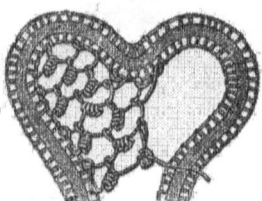

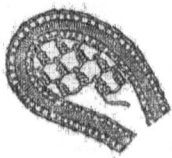

No. 30.—Point de Venise.

No. 31.—Point de Venise.

No. 32.—Point de Venise.

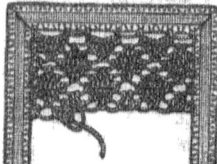

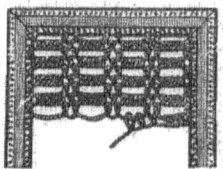

No. 33.—Point de Valenciennes.

No. 34.—Point de Grecque.

No. 35.—Point Brabançon.

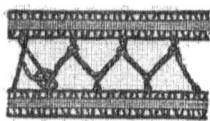

No. 36.—Point de Tulle.

No. 37.—Point d'Alençon, with Twisted Stitch.

No. 38.—Point de Fillet and Point de Reprise.

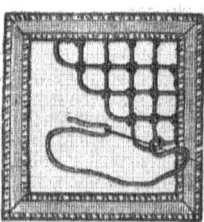

No. 39.—Point de Fillet (Net Groundwork Stitch).

No. 40.—Point de Cordova.

No. 41.—Point de Reprise.

No. 21.—PETIT POINT DE VENISE, OR LITTLE VENICE POINT.—This stitch is worked in the same manner as point de Venise, but one tight stitch only is worked in each loose button-hole stitch. This is a most useful stitch for filling in small spaces.

NOS. 22 TO 32.—BUTTON-HOLE STITCH BACKWARDS; POINT DE VENISE.—This effective button-hole looping consists of, first, a common button-hole stitch, as a kind of footing, and then a second looped into it, as shown in No. 39 on page 19, in point de fillet. No. 24 gives this stitch worked forwards and backwards as a pattern, with a line of plain button-hole stitches, forming a stripe pattern. No. 23 shows, in large size, the mode of working very beautiful point de Venise, either for an outer edge or for patterns, by looping three or four stitches into the first large button-hole stitch, which makes a thick scallop. No. 26 gives the edging in the size it would generally appear; No. 27, with the stitches farther apart; consequently the pattern is more open. No. 28 is worked from left to right, like Brussels point. Work 1 loose button-hole stitch, and in this stitch work 4 button-hole stitches tightly drawn up, then work another loose button-hole stitch, then four more tight button-hole stitches in the loose one; repeat to the end of the row, and fasten off. No. 29 is formed by joining the single button-hole stitch line in returning. No. 31 gives a pattern, with the same thick scallops worked forwards and backwards, and is very pretty as a guipure ground between thick arabesque patterns. By working downwards in the large button-hole scallop, the pattern represented in No. 32 is formed, which is equally pretty worked in single lines, for enclosing large patterns. The three patterns represented in Nos. 22, 25 and 30 are very similar; about two or three button-hole stitches are worked close together, downwards, as shown in the design. These also serve for enclosing patterns, or they may be arranged in the corded pattern, as the point d'Anvers, for thick patterns.

No. 33.—POINT DE VALENCIENNES, OR VALENCIENNES STITCH.—This stitch appears complicated, but it is really easy to work. Begin at the left hand and work 6 point de Bruxelles stitches at unequal distances, every alternate stitch being the larger.

Second row.—Upon the first large or long stitch work 9 close button-hole stitches, then 1 short point de Bruxelles stitch under the one above, then 9 close stitches, and so on to the end of the row.

Third row.—Make 5 close button-hole stitches in the 9 of previous row, 1 short point de Bruxelles, 2 close (in the Bruxelles stitch), 1 short point de Bruxelles, 5 close, 1 short point de Bruxelles, 2 close, 1 short, 5 close, 1 short and repeat.

Fourth row.—Make 5 close, 1 short point de Bruxelles, 2 close, 1 short, 5 close, 1 short, 2 close, 1 short and repeat. Continue the rows until sufficient of the pattern is worked.

No. 34.—POINT DE GRECQUE OR GRECIAN POINT.—Point de Grecque is made from left to right, and is worked backward and forward. It is begun by 1 stitch in loose point de Bruxelles and is followed by 3 of close point d'Espagne; then 1 Bruxelles, 3 point d'Espagne, to the end of the row; in returning work in the same manner.

No. 35.—POINT BRABANÇON.—This stitch is worked as follows, from left to right:—

First row.—Make 1 long, loose point de Bruxelles, and one short, loose one alternately to end of row.

Second row.—Make 7 tight point de Bruxelles in the 1 long, loose stitch, and 2 short, loose point de Bruxelles in the short, loose stitch on previous row, and repeat across the row.

Third row.—Same as first.

No. 36.—POINT DE TULLE.—This stitch is used as a ground-work for very fine work, and is worked in rows backward and forward in the same stitch as open point d'Espagne. When this is completed the work is gone over a second time by inserting the needle under one twisted bar, bringing it out and inserting it at + and bringing it out again at the dot. This produces a close double twist that is very effective.

No. 37.—POINT D'ALENÇON, WITH TWISTED STITCH.—This stitch is used to fill in narrow spaces where great lightness of effect is desired, and is usually seen along the sides of insertions and the tops of edgings. Plain point d'Alençon is worked over and under in bars in a sort of herring-bone pattern, and a twisted stitch is made as seen in the engraving, by twisting the thread three times around each bar and knotting it at the angles as pictured. The effect is similar to one of the drawn-work hem-stitches.

No. 38.—POINT DE FILLET AND POINT DE REPRISE.—The network seen in this engraving is the first stitch mentioned, while the block-work is the second. Both are clearly illustrated and need no written explanation of the methods employed in making them.

No. 39.—POINT DE FILLET, OR NET GROUNDWORK STITCH.—This stitch is also represented at No. 38 on page 19, but the method of making the knot is here illustrated. It is used for groundwork where Brussels net is not imitated, and is very effective wherever it is used. It is begun in the corner or crosswise of the space to be filled. A loose point de Bruxelles stitch is first taken and fastened to the braid, then passed twice through the braid, as shown in the illustration, and worked in rows backward and forward, as follows: 1 point de Bruxelles stitch, then before proceeding to the next stitch, pass the needle *under* the knot, *over* the thread, and again *under* it, as shown in the illustration. This stitch is very quickly worked.

No. 40.—POINT DE CORDOVA.—This stitch is useful as a variation, and resembles the point de reprise of guipure lace making. It is worked in a similar manner, over and under the sides of squares formed by intersecting straight lines of the thread.

No. 41.—POINT DE REPRISE.—This stitch is worked by darning over and under two threads forming a triangle. The space is filled by parallel and crosswise bars placed at equal distances, and on the triangles thus produced point de reprise is worked.

Nos. 42 to 48.—POINT D'ESPAGNE, OR SPANISH POINT.—This variety of stitch is worked from left to right, as follows (see No. 43): Insert the needle in the edge of the braid, keeping the thread turned to the right, and bringing it out inside the loop formed by the thread (see illustration); the needle must pass from the back of the loop entirely through it. Pass the needle under the stitch and bring it out in front, thus twice twisting the thread, which produces the cord-like appearance of this stitch. At the end of each row fasten to the braid and sew back, inserting the needle once in every open stitch. No. 48 shows how the length of the stitch and the number of the twists may be increased to suit the filling-in of an irregular space. No. 42 is worked like open point d'Espagne (see No. 43) but is made so closely as to only allow the needle to pass through in the next row. It is also worked from left to right, and is fastened to the braid at the end of each row. No. 44 is worked in exactly the same way as the open and close varieties just mentioned, as follows: 3 close stitches, 1 open, 3 close to the end of each row. Sew back, and in the next row make 1 open, 3 close, 1 open, 3 close to the end; repeat the rows as far as necessary, taking care that the close and open stitches follow in regular order. Diamonds, stars, squares blocks and various other pretty patterns may be formed with this stitch.

No. 49.—POINT D'ANGLETERRE (ENGLISH STITCH).—This lace is worked as follows: Cover the space to be filled in with lines of thread about an eighth of an inch apart, then form cross-lines, intersecting those already made and passing alternately under and over them; work a rosette on every spot where two lines cross by working over and under the two lines about 16 times round; then twist the threads twice round the ground-work thread, and begin to form another rosette at the crossing threads.

Wheels and rosettes are used to fill up spaces, or in combination, to form lace.

No. 50.—ROSETTE IN RAISED POINT D'ANGLETERRE.—This rosette is worked in a manner similar to the English wheel, the difference being that after each stitch is passed round and under the bars, the thread is passed loosely around in the reverse direction, as shown in the illustration, before proceeding to make the next stitch.

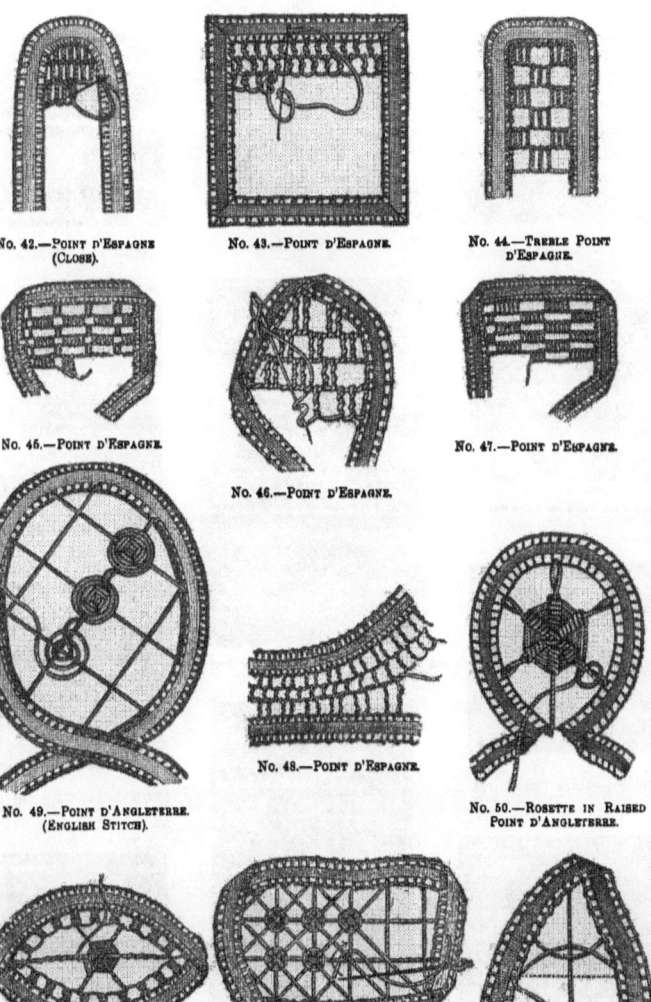

No. 42.—POINT D'ESPAGNE (CLOSE).

No. 43.—POINT D'ESPAGNE.

No. 44.—TREBLE POINT D'ESPAGNE.

No. 45.—POINT D'ESPAGNE.

No. 46.—POINT D'ESPAGNE.

No. 47.—POINT D'ESPAGNE.

No. 49.—POINT D'ANGLETERRE. (ENGLISH STITCH).

No. 48.—POINT D'ESPAGNE.

No. 50.—ROSETTE IN RAISED POINT D'ANGLETERRE.

No. 51.—SPINNING-WHEEL ROSETTE.

No 52.—POINT D'ANGLETERRE. (ROSETTE PATTERN).

No. 53.—POINT D'ANGLE-TERRE. (DETAIL.)

No. 54.—ITALIAN LACE STITCH.

No. 55.—ROSE POINT LACE-STITCH.

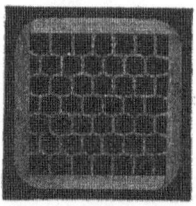

No. 56.—ITALIAN GROUND STITCH.

No. 57.—FLEMISH LACE STITCH.

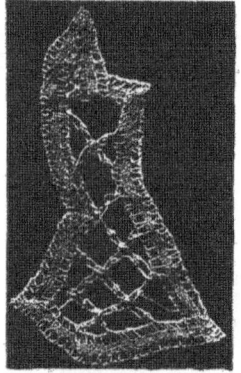

No. 58.—BRUGES LACE FILLING-IN STITCH.

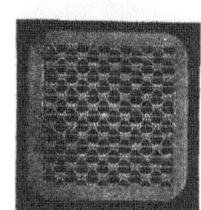

No. 59.—COBWEB LACE STITCH.

No. 60.—GENOA LACE STITCH.

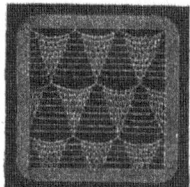

No. 61.—FAN LACE STITCH.

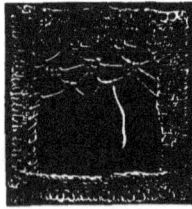

No. 62.—SPANISH-NET STITCH.

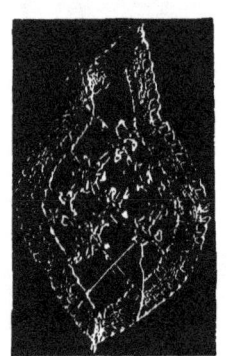

No. 63.—BRUGES LACE STITCH.

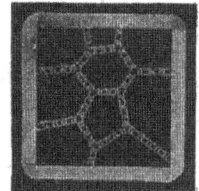

No. 64.—OPEN LACE BARS.

No. 51.—Spinning-Wheel Rosette.—These rosettes are very useful for filling the empty spaces in foundations or patterns. The engraving gives a wheel in which the thread is twisted over six thread bars in a line (point de Venise).

Nos. 52 and 53.—Point d'Angleterre: Rosette Pattern.—There are several kinds of rosette patterns, which, acording to the number of threads stretched across, require a looser or closer spinning-stitch for the wheels. The spaces must be most regularly and evenly arranged. For the rosettes in No. 49 the threads must be first of all stretched in one direction, then plaited through in the opposite direction; they are then worked in lines, according to design. The rosettes in the double trellis pattern, No. 52, have at first only one of the diagonal threads stretched across; the second slanting thread is placed in the working of the wheels, as shown in No. 52. Rosettes with loose thread-squares, represented in the bars at No. 78, page 27, are particularly intended for leaves. No. 53 shows the laying on of the first threads. No. 78 represents the work farther advanced.

The pattern is arranged over the first thread stretched across, which forms a kind of vein through the leaf; these rosettes may be used in their varieties for separate, middle or joining patterns.

No. 54.—Italian Lace Stitch (also Called Point d'Anvers.)—Commence at the right side and pass the thread to the left.

First row.—Make a loose button-hole stitch in the braid to form a loop, then pass the needle under the line of thread, making the loops an eighth of an inch apart.

Second row.—Pass the thread back to the left, make a button-hole stitch in every loop, and pass the needle under the line of thread after each button-hole stitch.

No. 55.—Rose Point Lace Stitch.—Make a foundation of single threads, crossing them to form the large squares. Work a button-hole stitch at each crossing to make it firm. Now begin at the top, at the right side and fill the first square with Brussels-net stitches, finishing at the lower left corner. Fill every alternate square in the same way as seen in the picture.

Now cross the open squares diagonally with two threads, twisting each thread around the adjoining one as represented. (Carry one thread across all the squares from corner to corner first; then twist back, fastening at the corner started from; cross these threads in the same way from the opposite direction). When twisting the thread back from the last set of crossings, make a rosette at each center crossing as follows: Keep the space open with a pin and trace round it with a darning movement five or six times; commence at the single thread and work a close button-hole stitch over the tracing entirely around, and then twist along the single thread to the center of the next square. This is a very effective design for spaces.

No. 56.—Italian Ground Stitch.—Commence at the left side, and work as follows: First row.—Make a loose button-hole stitch to form a loop a quarter of an inch wide, and then make a plain stitch into the loop to twist it, and continue to the end.

Second row.—Make two plain stitches into each loop, working back to the left.

Third row.—Repeat first row.

No. 57.—Flemish Lace Stitch.—Commence at the right side, and work as follows: First row.—Work two button-hole stitches close together, miss the space of 2, work 2, miss the space of 8; this will leave a large loop and a small one alternately.

Second row.—Make 8 button-hole stitches in the larger loops, and 2 in the small ones.

Third row.—Repeat the first row, making 2 stitches in each loop of the second row.

Nos. 58 and 63.—Bruges Lace Stitches.—These stitches are used only in making Bruges lace. No. 63 shows the stitch complete, while No. 58 shows the filling-in or foundation stitch, which is often used where light bars are needed. It is made as follows: Fasten the thread at one side of the braid, carry it across to the opposite side, fasten with a button-hole stitch and then make a second stitch about twice the thickness of the thread from the first one. Now work back on the crossing thread as follows: (Calculate about where the crossing threads which will come from the opposite direction will intersect, and arrange to have a button-hole stitch come between the intersections.) Having made the second stitch in the braid, make the first button-hole stitch on the line, but leave it loose enough so that you can take two other button-hole stitches across its loop, inserting the needle after the manner seen at No. 23, page 18, for each of the two stitches. Draw them tightly and that will make a knot like those seen between the crossings in No. 58. When the first end of the crossing thread is reached, fasten the thread and carry it along the braid to the point where you wish the second line to begin. Then carry to the other side parallel with the first line, and work back as before. When all the lines in this direction are made, cross them in the opposite direction to form the square, making the knots as before and also one at each crossing. When the stitch seen at No. 63 is desired, the rosette will have to be formed as you reach the intersections or crossings. Make the knot as directed, then run over and under the lines around the knot, in spider-web style, for two or three times and finish by making a knot at each side between the crossing threads. The effect of these two stitches may be seen in the scarf-end on page 55.

No. 59.—COBWEB LACE STITCH.—Commence at the right side, pass the thread to the left, work three button-hole stitches, miss the space of 3, which will leave a small loop, and continue these details to the end.

Second row.—Pass the thread back to the left side, work 3 button-hole stitches in each loop, taking up the line of thread with the loop, as seen in the engraving.

No. 60.—GENOA LACE STITCH.—Commence at the right side, and work as follows:

First row.—Work 4 button-hole stitches, miss the space of 3, work 3, miss the space of 3, work 4. Continue to the end.

Second row.—Work 9 stitches close together, three into the spaces of the 4, and 3 more into the loop at each side of it. Miss the 3 stitches, and make 9 as before.

Third row.—Make 9 close stitches, 3 into the last 3 spaces of the 9, 3 into the loop, and 3 into the first spaces of the 9 next, and so on to the end.

Fourth row.—Repeat the first, making the 3 stitches into the loop, and the 4 into the center spaces of the 9.

No. 61.—FAN LACE STITCH.—Commence at the right side, and work as follows:

First row.—Make 1 button-hole stitch and miss the space of 8, which will leave a long loop.

Second row.—Make 8 button-hole stitches in each loop.

Third row.—Make 7 stitches into the spaces between the 8, and so decrease one in every row until only one remains, as may be seen by referring to the illustration.

No. 62.—SPANISH NET STITCH.—The principle of this stitch is the same as that of the Turkish stitch seen at No. 20, page 18 that is, it is made with bars and button-hole stitches, and the loose bars are caught to the clusters of three with two button-hole stitches.

No. 64.—OPEN LACE BARS.—Pass a thread from right to left. Make it firm by working a second stitch into the braid; work 2 button-hole stitches on this line of thread, close together. Then work 1 button-hole stitch on the lower thread at the left-hand side, and draw it close to the 2 stitches on the line of thread. Miss the space of 2 and repeat.

NOS. 65 AND 67.—SORRENTO WHEEL.—This is worked by fastening the thread in the pattern to be filled up, as indicated by the letters. Fasten it first to the place *a*, then at place *b*, carrying it back to the middle of the first formed bar by winding it round; fasten again at *c*, carrying it back again to the center by winding it around the bar, and so on to all the letters; then work over and under the bars thus formed.

No. 66.—CHURCH STITCH.—This stitch is used alone for church lace. It is very simple,

No. 65.—SORRENTO WHEEL.

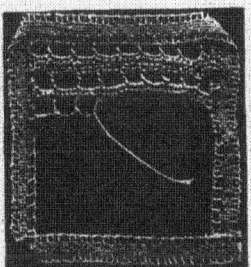

No. 66.—CHURCH LACE STITCH.

No. 67.—SORRENTO WHEEL.

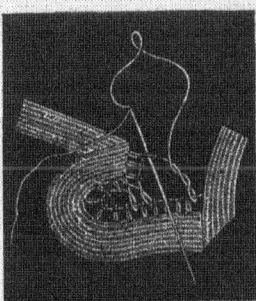

No. 68.—LIMOGES LACE STITCH.

No. 69.—PICOT.

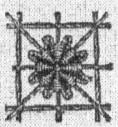

No. 70.—WHEEL
AND PICOT.

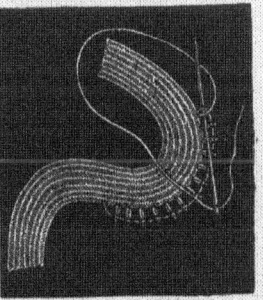

No. 71.—LIMOGES LACE STITCH.

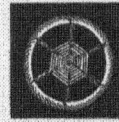

No. 72.—ENGLISH WHEEL.

No. 73.—MECHLIN LACE WHEEL.

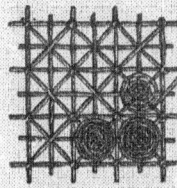

No. 74.—CLOSE ENGLISH
WHEELS.

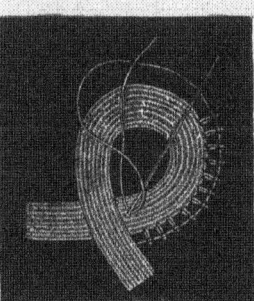

No. 75.—LIMOGES LACE STITCH.

No. 76.—THIRD METHOD OF
MAKING PICOTS OR DOTS.

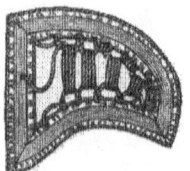 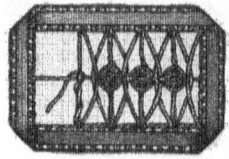 

No. 77.—D'Alençon Bars.　　No. 78.—Bars of Point d'Angleterre.　　No. 79.—Plain Venetian Bars.

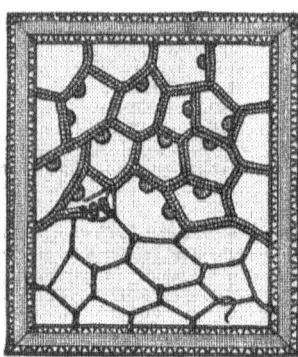

No. 80.—Raleigh Bars.

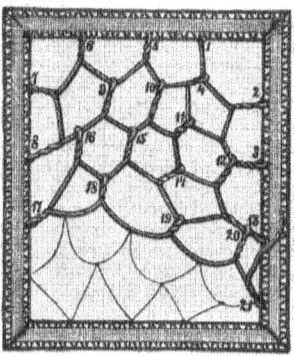

No. 81.—Network for Working Raleigh Bars.

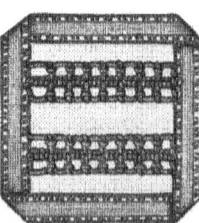 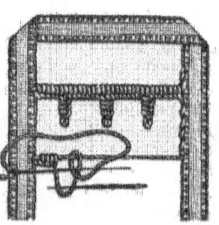 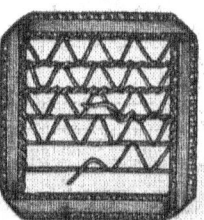

No. 82.—Point de Venise Bars
(Edged).

No. 83.—Dotted Point de
Venise Bars.

No. 84.—D'Alençon and
Sorrento Bars.

consisting only of button-hole stitches arranged as follows : Make the first row of stitches as seen in No. 1 on page 34. Then work a close row of button-hole stitches (as seen in the second row of No. 66); work back another row, but instead of taking the stitch *between* two stitches of the first row, take it through the *twist or loop* of a stitch. Work the third row in the same manner. Then repeat the first row of twisted loops and repeat also the three rows of button-hole stitches. The engraving shows the development of the work but is not a design. The twisted row and the three solid rows alternate in all designs.

Nos. 68, 71 AND 75.—LIMOGES LACE STITCH.—The peculiarity of Limoges lace consists in its being made with plain braid, and the edge is all worked to it. The braid is shown very greatly increased in size in the engravings 68, 71 and 75, which also show the proper mode of working the lace; the braid in the proper width is shown in No. 112 on page 86.

In working Limoges lace it is very important that the braid be soft and well made, and that the thread be of a suitable size and quality. In black (silk) materials it is equally as beautiful as in white, and better adapted for some purposes.

Tack the braid upon the design, holding it rather loosely, as the semi-transparency thus secured adds much to the beauty of the lace. Then run a very fine cotton through the whole length of the braid, carefully keeping it *inside* the curves, crossing from one edge of the braid to the other wherever the pattern demands it. The curves will then retain their exact shape when taken off the paper. When you come to a corner where the braid folds over, a few extra stitches will be required to make it neat and firm. Then commence the edge, which consists only of a loose button-hole stitch, with a tight one of the same kind in every loose one, so that the edge is entirely finished in one row. When you are edging the braid nearest to that already done, the bars must be introduced to connect them. This edge, with the bars, is also done in one row. When the braids so nearly touch as to leave no room for a bar, they should be joined by a herring-bone stitch.

When the space is so large that it must be filled up with a network of bars, instead of passing the needle through an opposite stitch, pass it round the middle of a neighboring bar, making a tight button-hole stitch upon the perfect bar to secure the one in progress in its proper place. Several bars may be made, when desired, by taking the single thread from bar to bar, or stitch to stitch, working the twisting round the already half-made bars as you return. The extra edge seen is only the same stitch as the ordinary edge, worked with *three tight stitches instead of one*. The little spot seen in several places is made thus : Make one bar across the space, and complete the second one (which crosses it) as far as the center, where the two bars touch each other : next darn round, under one thread and over another, until the spot is large enough, then finish the twisting round of the imperfect bar.

Nos. 69 AND 70.—PICOTS.—No. 69 also shows a very effective picot, which may be worked round the threads that cross each other or round a little spinning-stitch or wheel ; it may also be used for flowers. For this kind of picot make first a button-hole stitch round the netted cross, push the needle in it, and wind the cotton ten or twelve times round for one picot ; then carefully draw another button-hole stitch round the netted cross to fasten the finished picot and to prepare for the next. No. 70 represents a finished wheel surrounded with very pretty picots.

No. 72.—ENGLISH WHEEL.—This is worked in the same manner as Sorrento wheels, but instead of *winding* the thread over and under the bars, the needle is inserted under each bar, and brought out again between the thread and the last stitch; this produces a kind of button-hole stitch, and gives the square, firm appearance possessed by this wheel.

No. 73.—MECHLIN LACE WHEEL.—This is one of the prettiest stitches in point lace, but also one of the most difficult to work correctly. It is made thus : Work a number of diagonal bars in button-hole stitch on a single thread in one direction, then begin at the opposite side in the same way, and work 5 or 6 stitches past the spot where the two lines cross; pass the thread round the cross twice, under and over the thread to form a circle. Work in button-hole stitch half of one quarter, make a dot by putting a fine pin in the loop instead of drawing the thread tight, and work 3 button-hole stitches in the loop held open by the pin, then take the pin out and continue as before. Beginners will do well to omit the dot, leaving the loop only on the wheel. Mechlin wheels are also worked in rows upon horizontal and parallel lines of thread.

No. 74.—CLOSE ENGLISH WHEELS.—These wheels may be used in open spaces and may be very easily made from the engraving. They are much like the wheels used in drawn work—indeed, many of the stitches used in lace are identical with those used in drawn-work.

No. 76.—THIRD METHOD OF MAKING PICOTS OR DOTS.—This method will be fully described in connection with the making of the Raleigh Bars seen at Nos. 80 and 81, page 27, and requires no description at this point. All dots and picots render work much more effective, and may be introduced at will by the worker.

The word "Bar" is applied to the many stitches used to connect the various parts of lace, and the beauty of the work depends greatly upon the class of bar selected and its suitability to the lace stitches used.

No. 77.—D'ALENÇON BARS.—These bars are worked upon point de Bruxelles edging, and are only applied to the inner part of a pattern, never being used as ground-work bars. The thread is merely passed three times over and under the point de Bruxelles stitches, the length of these bars being regulated by the space to be filled; when the third bar is completed a tight point de Bruxelles stitch fastens off the bars, and the thread is passed through the next point de Bruxelles stitch.

No. 78.—BARS OF POINT D'ANGLETERRE.—These bars may be worked singly or to fill up a space, as in the illustration. Work rosettes as in point d'Angleterre; when each rosette is finished twist the thread up the foundation thread to the top, fasten with one stitch, then pass it under the parallel line running through the center and over into the opposite braid; repeat on each side of each rosette, inserting the threads as seen in the illustration.

No. 79.—PLAIN VENETIAN BARS.—These bars are worked so as to form squares, triangles, etc., in button-hole stitch upon a straight thread.

The arrow in the illustration points to the direction for working the next stitch.

Nos. 80 AND 81.—RALEIGH BARS.—These bars are much used in making Battenburg lace and are very effective. They are worked over a foundation or network of coarse thread, and are twisted in places so that they will more easily fall into the desired form.

By following the numbering from 1 to 21 in No. 81, a square place may be easily filled, and portions of this arrangement applied to form groundwork of any shape desired. Upon this groundwork tight point de Bruxelles stitches are made, and the dot is worked upon these in one of the following ways:

DOTS OR PICOTS.—First Method.—Make 5 tight point de Bruxelles stitches, 1 loose point de Bruxelles; pass the needle under the loop and over the thread, as shown in point de Venise bars at No. 83, page 27, and draw up, leaving a small, open loop as in tatting. Work 5 tight point de Bruxelles stitches, and repeat.

Second Method.—Proceed as above directed, but instead of continuing the tight stitches, work two or three tight stitches in the loop thus formed and repeat.

Third Method.—Work 4 tight point de Bruxelles stitches; 1 loose, through which pass the needle point, wind the thread three or four times round the point (see No 76, page 26), press the thumb tightly on this, and draw the needle and thread through the twists. This is a quick mode of making the picot, and imitates most closely the real Spanish lace.

Illustration No. 76, page 26, also shows how this stitch may also be applied as a *regular* groundwork, but the beauty of old point groundwork bars consists in variety of form.

No. 82.—POINT DE VENISE BARS (EDGED).—Begin at the right hand and stretch a line of thread to the left side of the braid, fastening it with one tight stitch of point de Bruxelles. Upon this line work a succession of tight point de Bruxelles stitches. Then in every third stitch work one point de Venise stitch.

No. 83.—DOTTED POINT DE VENISE BARS.—These pretty bars are worked as follows: Stretch the thread from right to left; on this work 5 tight stitches of point de Bruxelles, then insert a pin in this last stitch to hold it open and loose, pass the needle under the loose stitch and over the thread, as clearly shown in the illustration, and in this loop work 3 tight point de Bruxelles stitches. Then work 5 more stitches and repeat to end of row.

The making of the dots or purls before mentioned as picots, is an important feature in bar work. All three names are employed for the same class of stitch.

No. 84.—D'ALENÇON AND SORRENTO BARS.—At Nos. 89 and 96 (this page), a description of the method of making Sorrento bars is given, while at No. 37 (page 20), is a description of plain and fancy d'Alençon stitches. The two methods are combined in the work seen at No. 84 where the process is so clearly illustrated that a mere novice in lace-work could not fail to produce it perfectly. The combined stitch is used in filling in spaces, etc.

Nos. 85, 86, 87, 88, AND 91, 93, 94 AND 95.—LOOSE AND TWISTED BARS: POINT D'ALENÇON.—No. 95 is a fine herring-bone stitch. The single cross-stitch, in very narrow spaces, must be worked into the braid. No. 93 represents the double cross-stitch consisting of two lines lying over each other. No. 94 gives the same stitch, fastened by a button-hole stitch made across it. In No. 91 the thread, which is carried plain across to the opposite side, is for the joining ; in returning it is twisted several times, according to the breadth, and these bars are repeated singly or in groups of two or three and four in the large spaces. According to No. 85, these bars are worked, like the cross-stitch, along both sides. (No. 77 on page 27, gives loose bars in bunches, worked in the button-hole edge, which are also very effective arranged at greater distances.) No. 87 represents the same bars twisted. This mode of joining is particularly desirable when the spaces suddenly increase or decrease in distance. In working Nos. 86 and 88 stretch a thread across, work it over, returning with a few button-hole stitches, and then wind the thread again through, according to No. 88. Where loose and firm bars are placed alternately—according to No. 86—there are always at least three, if not five, threads stretched across, and worked over very closely with the button-hole stitch (point d'esprit); in working these, the cross bars branch off from the principal bars, and may be ornamented with picots.

Nos. 89 AND 96.—SORRENTO BARS.— Each of the bars is worked from right to left, a straight thread being carried across and fastened securely with a stitch. The return consists of a simple twist under and over the straight thread ; three of these bars are usually placed close together at equal distances between the groups. The thread is sewed carefully over the braid in passing from one spot to another.

Nos. 90 AND 92.—VENETIAN BARS.—The bar at No. 90 is so simple that it really needs no description. It is worked over two straight threads in reverse button-hole stitch. No. 92 shows the Venetian bar used as the veining of a leaf and worked upon Sorrento bars.

No. 97.—POINT GRECQUE BARS.—These bars are so simply made that they are great favorites with beginners. They are begun at the top of the point, one straight thread being carried to the bottom; then the cross bars are worked after the method seen in the illustration.

No. 98.—ROSETTE BARS.—These bars have a pretty effect in joining ; they belong to the class of rosettes or spinning-stitches.

No. 99.—PICOT OR DOT ON SORRENTO BAR.—This dot is worked between rows of point de Bruxelles, 3 twisted stitches being worked into the loop left by the twisted thread.

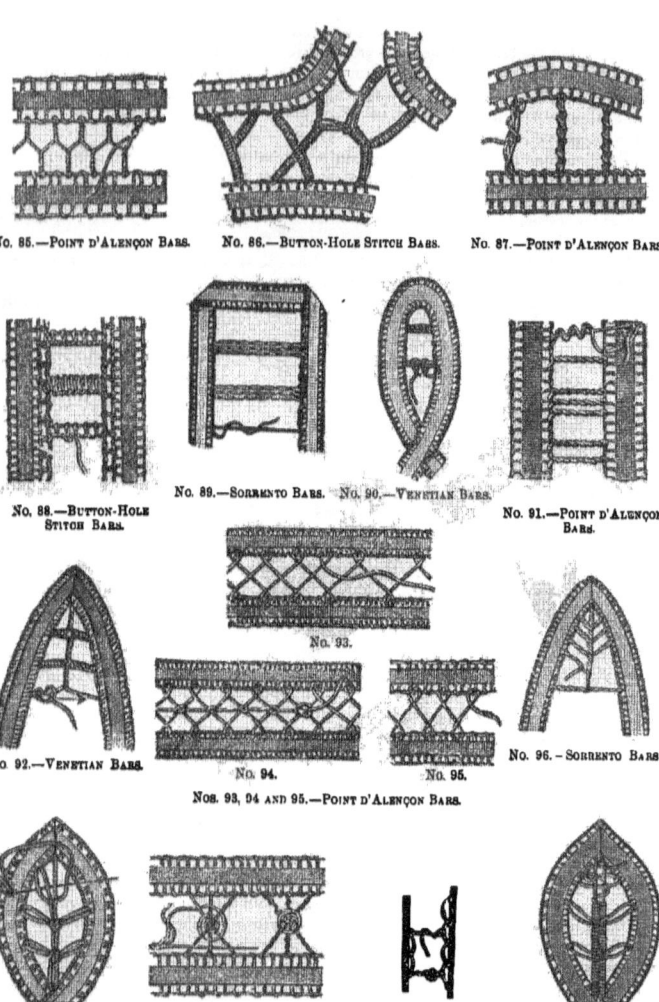

No. 85.—POINT D'ALENÇON BARS.   No. 86.—BUTTON-HOLE STITCH BARS.   No. 87.—POINT D'ALENÇON BARS.

No. 89.—SORRENTO BARS.   No. 90.—VENETIAN BARS.

No. 88.—BUTTON-HOLE STITCH BARS.

No. 91.—POINT D'ALENÇON BARS.

No. 93.

No. 92.—VENETIAN BARS.   No. 94.   No. 95.   No. 96.—SORRENTO BARS.

NOS. 93, 94 AND 95.—POINT D'ALENÇON BARS.

No. 98.—ROSETTE BARS.   No. 99.—PICOT OR DOT ON SORRENTO BAR.

No. 97.—POINT GRECQUE BARS.   No. 100.—POINT D'ANVERS BARS.

No. 100.—POINT D'ANVERS BARS.—Two upright bars form the foundation. The thread is carried over and under them as seen in the engraving, the side loops being added by the method depicted at the top of the point. The over and under work in point d'Anvers bars, without the side loops, is often used for plain bars for filling in odd spaces or wheels in heavy lace.

No. 101.—DOUBLE LEAF WITH VEIN.—The pattern of the leaf on the left is in point d'Espagne; that on the right is in loose point de Bruxelles, and has a vein. Such patterns, without reference to the kind of stitches, are called point de Valenciennes.

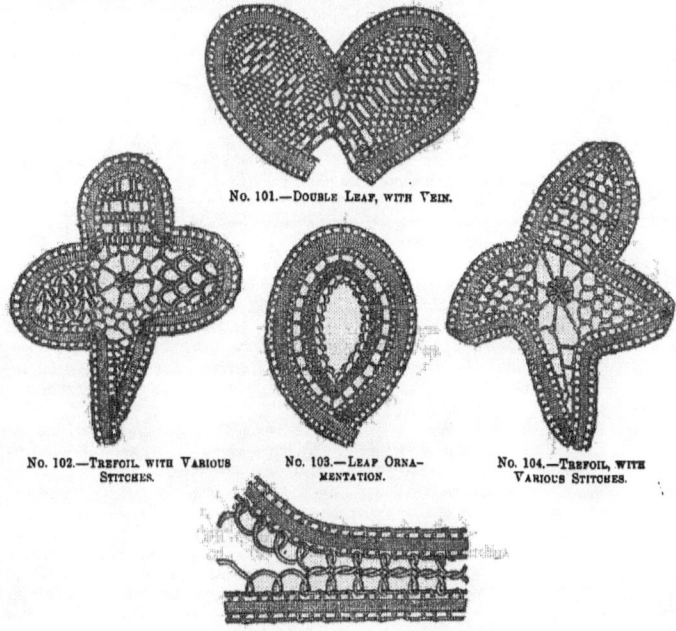

No. 101.—DOUBLE LEAF, WITH VEIN.

No. 102.—TREFOIL WITH VARIOUS STITCHES.

No. 103.—LEAF ORNAMENTATION.

No. 104.—TREFOIL, WITH VARIOUS STITCHES.

No. 105.—FESTOON JOINING: POINT D'ESPRIT.

Nos. 102 AND 104.—TREFOILS WITH SEVERAL PATTERNS.—These are only guides to show how the separate divisions of large leaves may be filled up with various lace-stitches, and joined together in the middle with a wheel, star, etc. Such stars or wheels may be worked in any of the various lace-stitches of the designs already explained.

No. 103.—LEAF ORNAMENTATION.—This consists of a row of point d'Espagne, enclosed by a very thick stripe of point de Bruxelles, with always four button-hole stitches in one point d'Espagne stitch. A line of point de Venise in thick scollops forms the inner edge.

No. 105.—FESTOON JOINING.—Simple button-hole stitches are looped into each other, and where the braid opens wider, the spinning-stitch, wheels, etc., may be inserted.

STITCHES FOR FILLING IN ROSETTES, OVALS AND SQUARES.

Nos. 1, 2, 3, 4, 5 AND 6.—BUTTON-HOLE STITCH BARS.—The principal parts of a great number of lace stitches consist of the common and the twisted button-hole stitch (point d'Espagne), in which more or less close, short, or long bars are worked, and round these one or more patterns are looped for a finish. The button-hole stitch bars of an open edge must be short and rather tightly twisted, that they may be worked round by any lace pattern.

No. 1 shows the working of this edge; No. 6 the cording; at the finish of this the thread must be tightly drawn and fastened. Upon this inner edge the lace work is again carried on; in every case, however, the thread is at last looped onto the first single bar, and is wound back to the edge, where it is fastened. No. 3 is a rosette with bars, with an open ring, and a button-hole edge round the ring; the button-hole stitch loops are drawn rather long, and the thread is wound several times through. No. 5 is a treble rosette (twisted button-hole stitch), with the ring filled up. Work two lines of the bars according to No. 2, and then work button-hole stitch round the middle edge. No. 4 shows No. 5 finished.

Nos. 7 AND 9.—SPINNING-STITCH OR WHEELS.—These are made by drawing the thread round through the lengthened middle point of the stretched threads. The mode of weaving in the thread is clearly shown in No. 7. No. 9 shows the finished wheel.

Nos. 15 AND 10.—OPEN WREATH ROSETTE.—The rosette is shown in a greatly increased size in No. 15, so that the mode of working the spinning-wheels over the foundation of corded button-hole bars is very apparent, and will be found to be very easy to work.

Nos. 11, 13, 14 AND 18.—PYRAMID ROSETTES AND OVALS.—The foundation for the rosettes is shown in No. 18. They are worked in point de reprise. No. 11 shows a finished pyramid rosette; No. 13 a pyramid oval.

Nos. 8, 12 AND 37.—OVALS IN POINT ALENÇON.—These ovals give varieties for filling in, and will be readily worked from the ovals in increased size, which, if carefully studied, will be found to be much easier than working from directions.

Nos. 16, 17 AND 19.—WHEELS WITH THREAD BARS.—A single thread is stretched across, and the work is carried on over the opening, and by cording along the edge. No. 16 shows the mode of stretching the threads across. After having stretched the third thread across, which gives six thread bars, carry the last thread only as far as the middle, and there bend out the cross threads, and draw them round once or twice more with the working-thread, in order to be able to work a firm open ring in point d'esprit, as shown in No. 17. The thread that is wanting is supplied at the last. No. 19 is a wheel with the thick round pattern in the center and has fourteen single-thread bars; the raised round in the center may be either in chain-stitch or a little woven wheel. In the middle of the space to be filled, work a stitch or a cross upon the plain under ground. These centers serve to stretch the loose thread loops.

Nos. 20 AND 21.—TREFOIL ROSETTE.—No. 25 shows the foundation for trefoil and bow rosettes. By winding the thread round the bar of the last bow the middle is reached, where all three bows are firmly drawn together before the leaf is filled up with the common point de reprise.

Nos. 22, 27 AND 28.—CROSS ROSETTE.—After the stretched thread bows, according to No. 22, are united by a thread ring, the helping cross in the middle must be taken away, and the rosette completed with darning and thick cross-stitches.

STITCHES FOR FILLING IN ROSETTES, OVALS AND SQUARES.

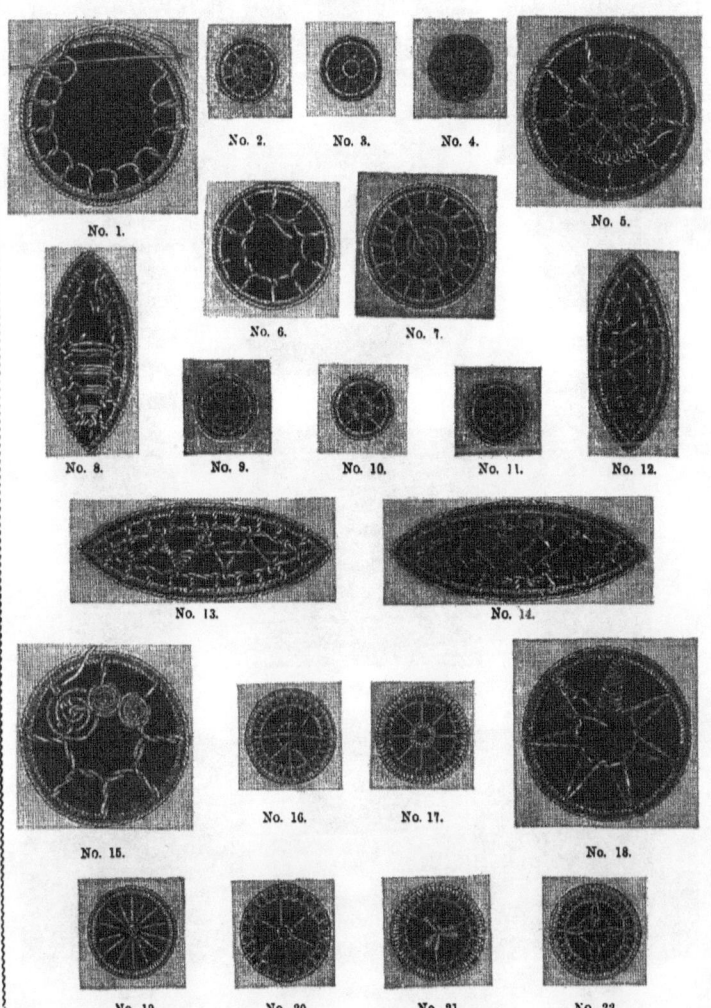

No. 1. No. 2. No. 3. No. 4. No. 5. No. 6. No. 7. No. 8. No. 9. No. 10. No. 11. No. 12. No. 13. No. 14. No. 15. No. 16. No. 17. No. 18. No. 19. No. 20. No. 21. No. 22.

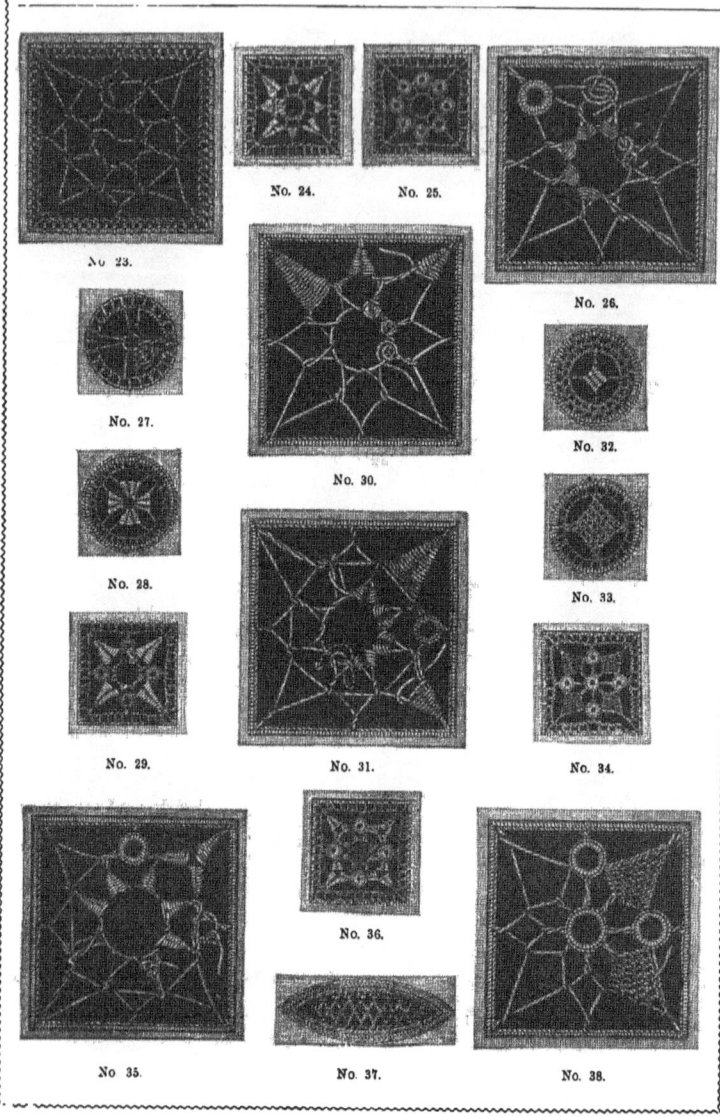

No. 23.

No. 24.　　No. 25.

No. 26.

No. 27.

No. 32.

No. 30.

No. 28.

No. 33.

No. 29.

No. 31.

No. 34.

No. 36.

No 35.

No. 37.

No. 38.

NOS. 24 AND 30.—SQUARE, WITH PYRAMID SCOLLOPS AND INTERWOVEN WHEELS.—
The threads are stretched across as before described, and the wheels are interwoven into the
inner triangle (No. 30). The outer edge consists of large and small pyramids interwoven,
as shown in design.

NOS. 25 AND 26.—SQUARE, WITH RINGS IN POINT D'ESPRIT, AND PATTERNS OF
CROSS-STITCHES.—The stretched thread must be fastened with the thread drawn through,
without the first loop row shown in No. 23; the second inner row is stretched across, and
worked inside, with thick patterns of cross-stitches. At the outer edge are rings in point
d'esprit, which join the working-thread. These rings extend from one to the other, forming
a circle.

NOS. 29 AND 31.—SQUARE, WITH PYRAMID SCOLLOPS, POINT D'ESPRIT RINGS, AND
PATTERNS OF CROSS-STITCHES.—The threads are stretched across according to No. 23, then
worked according to No. 31; with the same thread is worked a thick pattern of eight or
twelve cross-stitches, lying over each other in each of the little middle triangles, as shown
graduated in No. 31. The thread must be laid on afresh for the outer edge, and then a
pyramid and a ring worked alternately. The finished square is shown in No. 29.

NO. 32.—ROSETTE SQUARE.—For this, two bows are required, which are corded and
then joined with close cross-stitches, in the form of a little square.

NO. 33.—ROSETTE WITH SQUARE, FASTENED WITH BUTTON-HOLE STITCH.—The
outline of the square is worked with four button-hole stitches in the open edge, and this is
filled up in point d'Anvers, in which the square is again corded all round, and ornamented in
the corners with little thick rounds.

NOS. 34 AND 38.—SQUARE, WITH RINGS IN POINT D'ESPRIT AND OPEN SCOLLOPS.—
The stretching of the thread differs from No. 23 in the second row, in adding which the
inner space is narrowed off to a ring, which is closely worked in point d'esprit, uniting eight
radii, forming a star.

As shown in design, the outer edge consists of alternately point d'Espagne scollops
and rings in point d'esprit. These may be easily worked from No. 38, and must be
corded with the thread after they are looped on, so that the next ring may be joined on
immediately.

NOS. 35 AND 36.—SQUARE, WITH PYRAMID SCOLLOPS AND POINT D'ESPRIT RINGS.—
For this, two single loop-lines, with the thread drawn once through for a firm edge, must
be worked into each other, exactly according to No. 23, and then according to No. 31;
the middle triangles are filled up with single, and the large corner openings with three
pyramid scollops. In the four spaces of the outer edge between the corners, adjoining the
corner pattern, the rings are worked in point d'esprit. For the mode of working these, see
No. 26.

ROYAL BATTENBURG TEA-CLOTH AWARDED FIRST PRIZE
AT WORLD'S FAIR.

(See Frontispiece, page 6).

This beautiful tea-cloth, made by Miss Sara Hadley, of No. 923 Broadway, New York City,
is about a yard and a half square and has a center of rich, ivory-white, heavy satin. The border
is of Royal Battenburg lace and is in grape design with groups of buttons (see No. 2, page
12), representing the clusters of grapes, while broad Battenburg braid is used to outline the
vines and leaves. A network of fine stitches fills in the leaves, while the entire design is connected by Raleigh bars and Battenburg cord.

DESIGNS, LACE ARTICLES, EDGINGS, INSERTIONS, ETC., IN MODERN LACE.

(See Next and Following Pages).

HE designs and specimens given on this and the following pages, though smaller than the articles they represent, afford a correct idea of the method of making and the beauty of, Modern Lace, and also its adaptability to dainty accessories of the toilet and the household. Any design desired can be obtained from any lace-making establishment in any size, width or shape, according to the requirements of the article or lace to be made, and individual taste. Ingenious students will no doubt be able to adapt for themselves the designs offered, but it is not advisable for those who have not talent in the matter of drawing or designing to undertake an elaborate adaptation, though they may easily accomplish a simple one. Besides, a professional designer will furnish the design for a moderate sum, perfectly outlined upon tracing cloth, with ink, and with the proper filling-in stitches perfectly delineated; and if the student wishes it, will select the thread and braid appropriate for the design; or the student may select the braid she fancies, and the designer will then select the thread suitable for the braid.

The design for a point lace handkerchief is given in order to show the effect and arrangement of a design ready for working, as sent out from the lace-maker's. By a reference to the various stitches illustrated on the preceding pages, the stitches shown in one corner of the design may be readily identified. The following engraving shows how braid is applied to a design before the stitches are begun.

METHOD OF PLACING BRAID UPON DESIGNS.

(See Illustration at No. 2, page 38).

This illustration shows the method of arranging braid upon designs for Modern Lace, and how, after the braid is basted along the pattern, the tracing cloth is basted to *toile cirée* or to smooth, light brown wrapping paper to provide sufficient firmness for working.

The following instructions apply particularly to engraving No. 2, but their principle should be observed and applied to any design decided upon, as good results in lace-making largely depend upon the arrangement of the braid.

Run on a straight line of braid for the lower edge, with fine stitches, working as shown, from left to right. Take another piece of braid, or the other end of the same piece, and begin to lay the braid by "running" stitches in its center, keeping it as smooth and even as possible. The outer edge presents no difficulty, but the inner edge will not lie evenly without being drawn in by a needle and thread, as follows: Fasten whipping thread securely, and insert the needle in and out of the edge of the braid, as if for fine gathering; this thread when drawn up will keep the braid in its place. Two or three fastening-off stitches should be worked when each circle, half circle, or rounded curve of a pattern is finished, as the drawing or gathering thread remains in the work, and forms an important, though unseen, part of its structure.

Before cutting off the braid run a few stitches across it to prevent it from widening. Joins should be avoided, but when a join is necessary, stitch the braid together, open and turn back the ends, and stitch each portion down separately. When passing the thread from one part to another, run it along the center of the braid, allowing the stitches to show as little as possible. In commencing, make a few stitches, leaving the end of the thread on the wrong side and cutting it off afterwards. In fastening off, make a tight buttonhole stitch, run in three stitches, bring the needle out at the back, and cut off the thread.

Designs, Lace Articles, Edgings, Insertions, etc., in Modern Lace.

No. 1.—Design for a Lace Handkerchief Showing Stitches Partially Filled in.

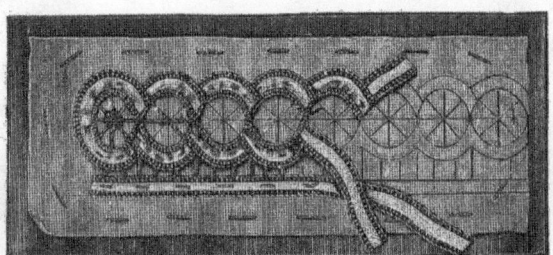

No 2.— Method of Placing Braid Upon Designs.

(A Description of the Method appears upon Page 37.)

No. 3.—Table-Square in Linen and Modern Lace.

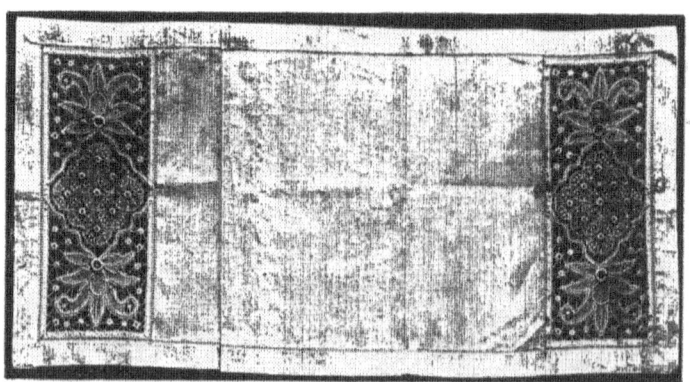

No. 4.—Buffet-Scarf in Linen and Modern Lace.

No. 5.—Corner of Tea-Cloth with Battenburg Border.

No. 6.—Point Lace Finger-Bowl Doily.

No. 7.—Punch-Glass Doily of Lawn and Needle-Honiton Lace.

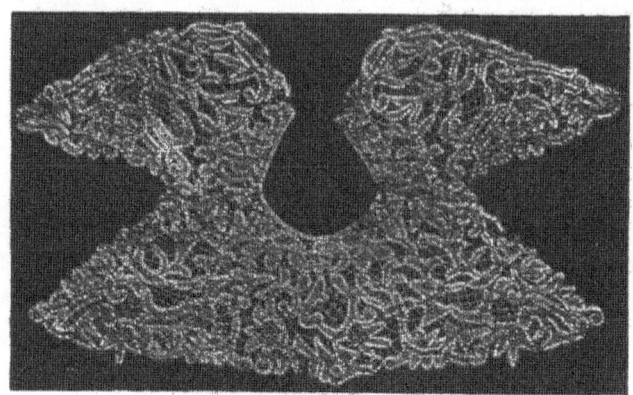

No. 8.—COLLAR IN MODERN LACE.

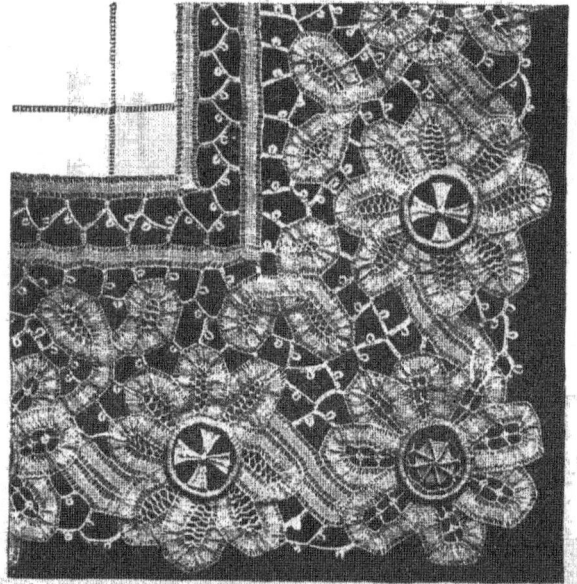

No. 9.—BORDER AND CORNER FOR TABLE-SQUARE IN BATTENBURG LACE.

No. 10.—INFANT'S BIB IN MODERN LACE.

No. 11.—DESIGN IN HONITON LACE.

No. 12.—Square of Needle-Honiton and Drawn-Work.

No. 13.—Punch-Glass Doily in Point Lace.

No. 14.—Battenburg Lace Finger-Bowl Doily.

No. 15.—CENTER-PIECE, WITH BATTENBURG LACE BORDER.

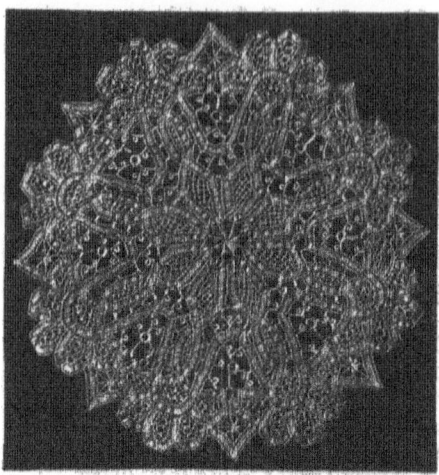

No. 16.—Finger-Bowl Doily of Battenburg Lace.

No. 17.—Modern Lace Edging.

No. 18.—Design for Point Lace Handkerchief.

No. 19.—Corner of Battenburg Lace for Tea-Cloth.

No. 20.—Finger-Bowl Doily of Ideal Honiton and Linen Lawn.

No. 21.—Old Bruges Lace Edging.

No. 22.—Corner of Honiton Lace Handkerchief.

No. 23.—Design in Point de Bruges.

No. 24.—Handkerchief of Honiton and Point Lace.

No. 25.—Ideal Honiton Finger-Bowl Doily.

No. 26.—Corner in Modern Lace.

4

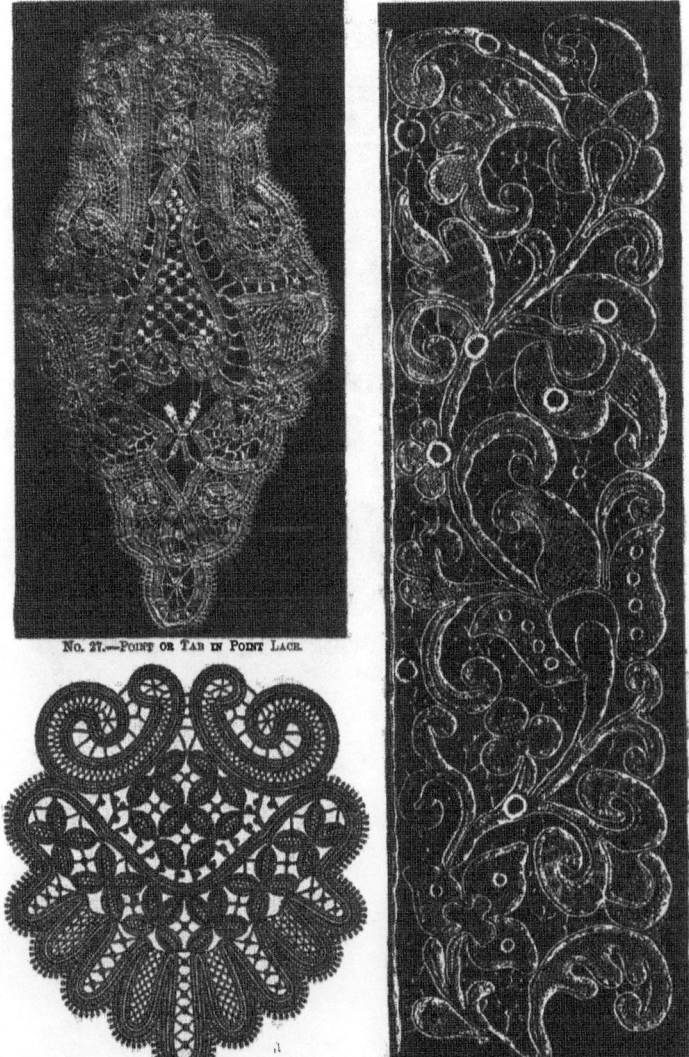

No. 27.—POINT OR TAB IN POINT LACE.

No. 28.—SCARF-END IN POINT AND HONITON LACE.

No. 29.—MODERN VENETIAN POINT.

No. 30.—MODERN LACE.

No. 32.—Finger-Bowl Doily of Ideal Honiton Lace and Linen Lawn (Almost Full Size).

No. 33.—Ideal Honiton Finger-Bowl Doily.

No. 34.—Ideal Honiton Finger-Bowl Doily.

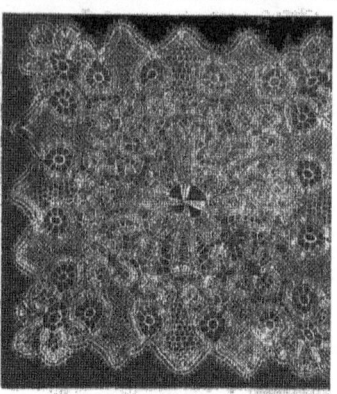

NO. 35.—POINT LACE FINGER-BOWL DOILY.

NO. 36.—POINT LACE FINGER-BOWL DOILY.

NO. 37.—CENTER-PIECE FOR ROUND TABLE. (LINEN AND BATTENBURG LACE.)

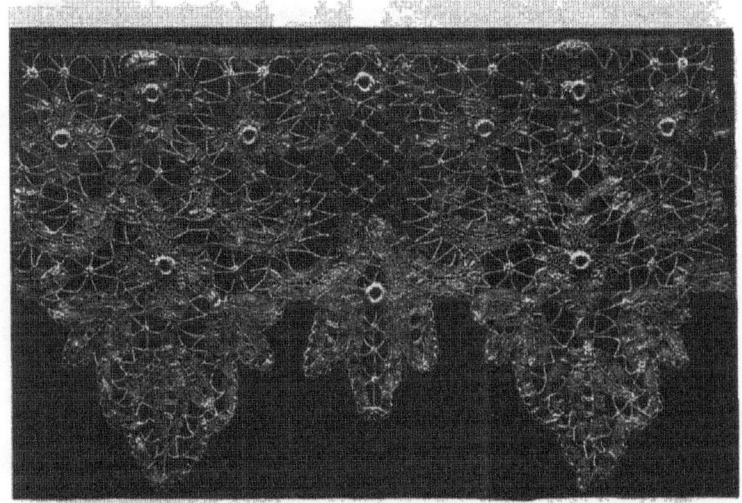

No. 38.—Design in Renaissance Lace.

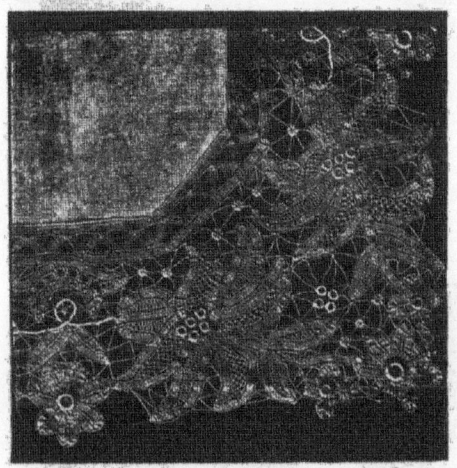

No. 39.—Corner of Table-Square, with Battenburg Border.

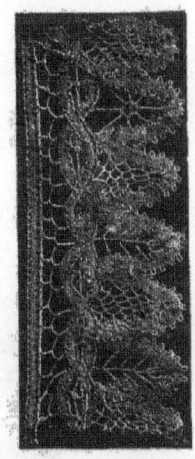

No 40.—Narrow Modern Lace.

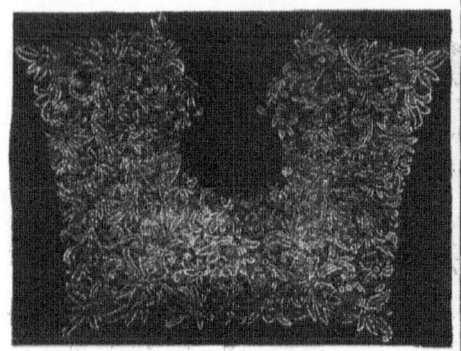

NO. 41.—BATTENBURG LACE COLLAR.

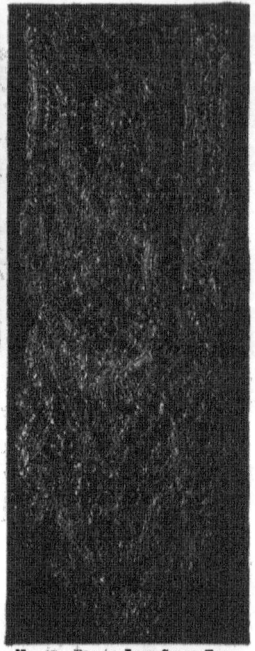

NO. 43.—BRUGES LACE SCARF-END.

NO. 42.—DESIGN FOR LACE COLLAR.

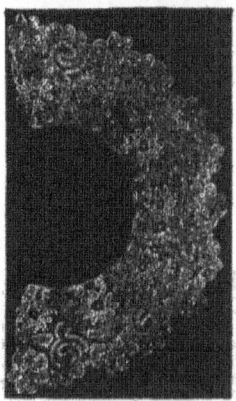

NO. 44.—PRINCESS LACE COLLAR.

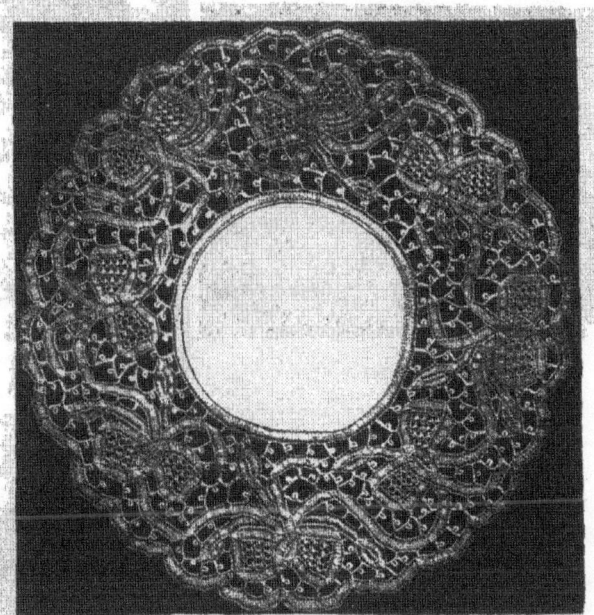

No. 45.—Plate-Doily with Battenburg Border.

No. 46.—Design for Insertion in Battenburg Lace.

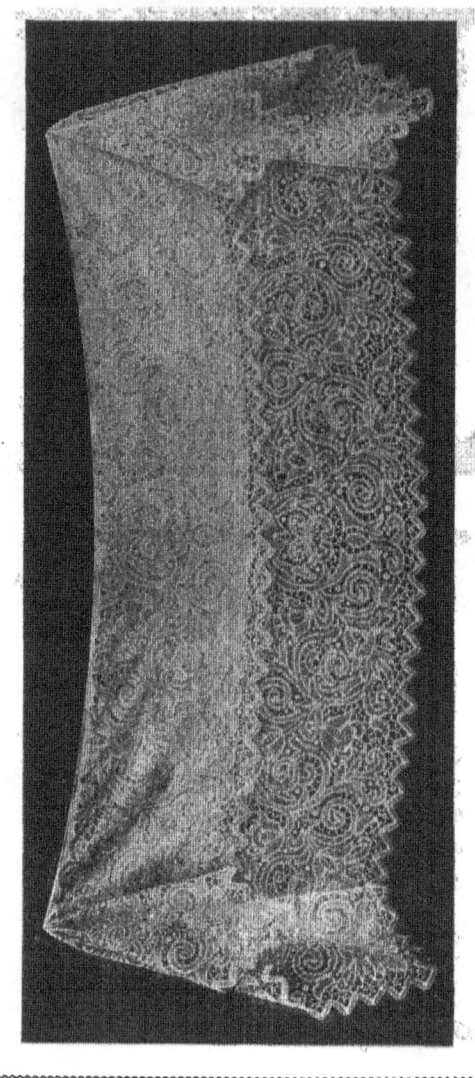

NO. 47.—TABLE-RUNNER WITH NEEDLE-POINT BORDER. (RECEIVED FIRST PRIZE AT WORLD'S FAIR.)

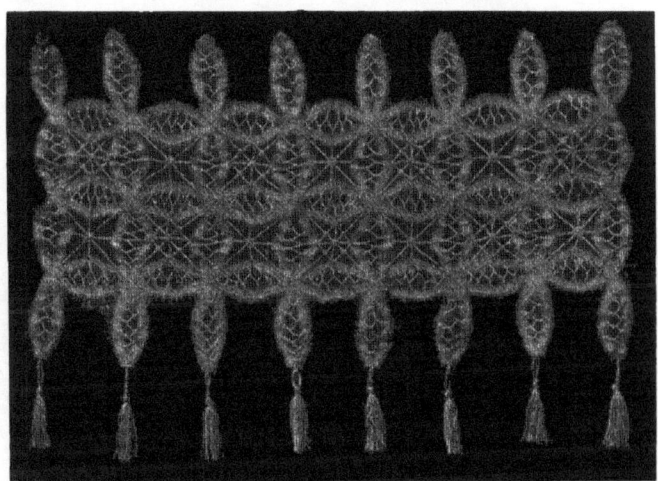

No. 48.—Tidy of Ribbon Lace.

No. 49.—Design for Battenburg Lace.

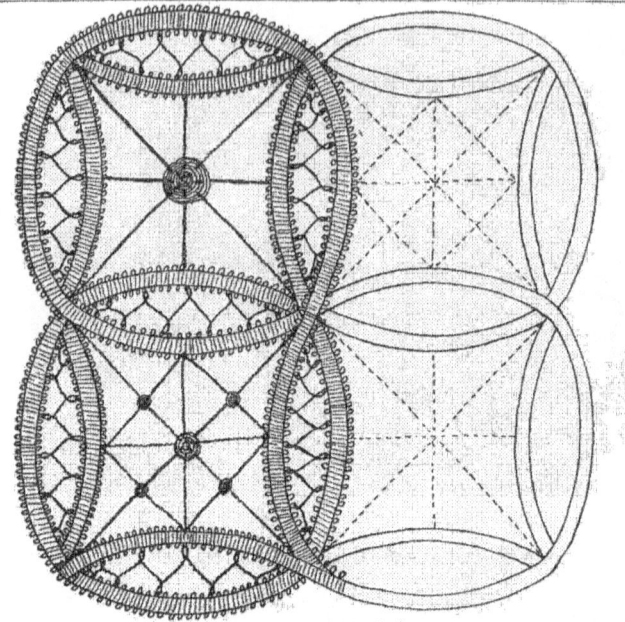

No. 50.—Detail for Ribbon Lace.

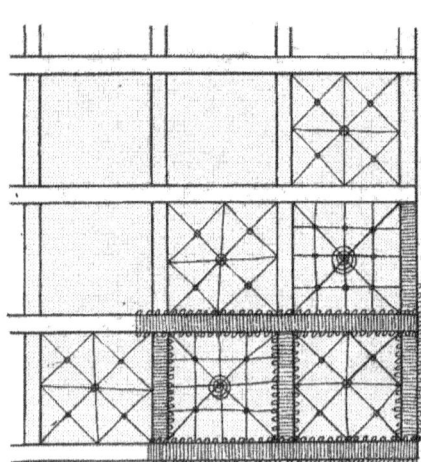

No. 51.—Square Design for Ribbon Lace.

No. 52.—Design in Modern Lace.

No. 54.—Modern-Point Lace Edging.

No. 53.—Royal Battenburg Edging.   No. 55.—Design for Collar in Battenburg Lace.

No. 56.—DESIGN FOR A CORNER IN BATTENBURG LACE.

No. 57.—BUTTERFLY DESIGN FOR FINE BATTENBURG LACE.

No. 58.—DESIGN IN MODERN LACE.

No. 59.—CORNER OF SQUARE IN MODERN LACE.

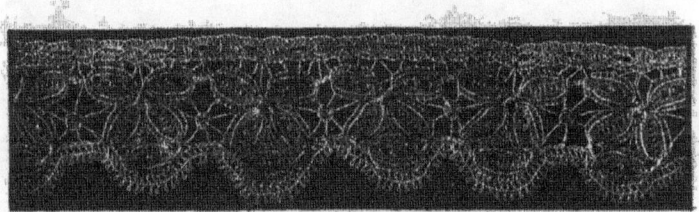

No. 60.—HONITON EDGING.

No. 61.—Finger-Bowl Doily in Battenburg Lace.

No. 62.—Design in Modern Lace.

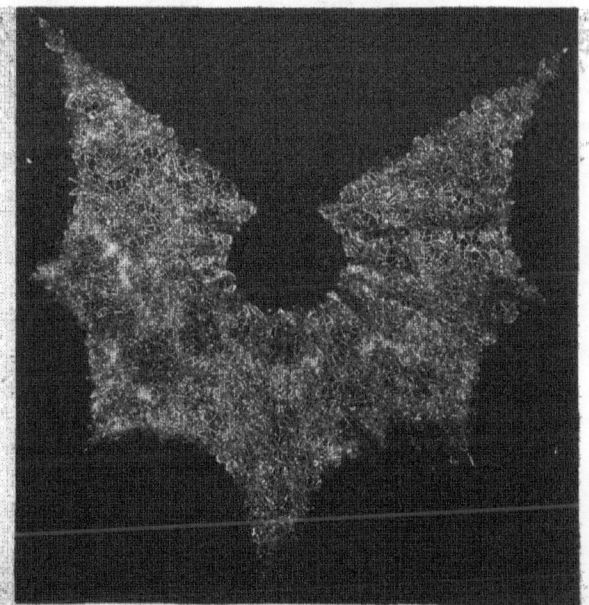

No. 63.—STAR-POINTED BATTENBURG LACE CAPE.

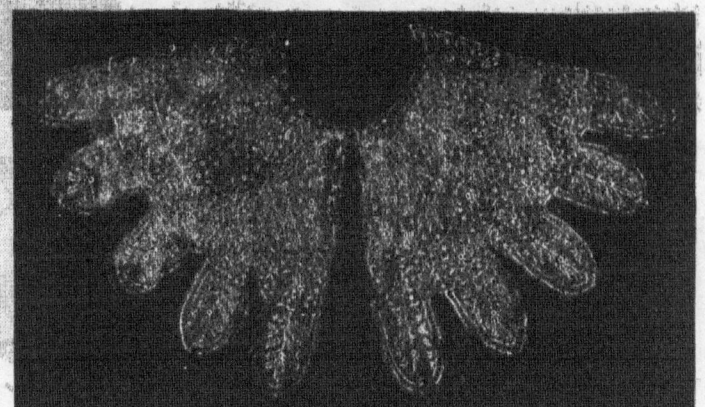

No. 64.—CIRCULAR BATTENBURG LACE CAPE.

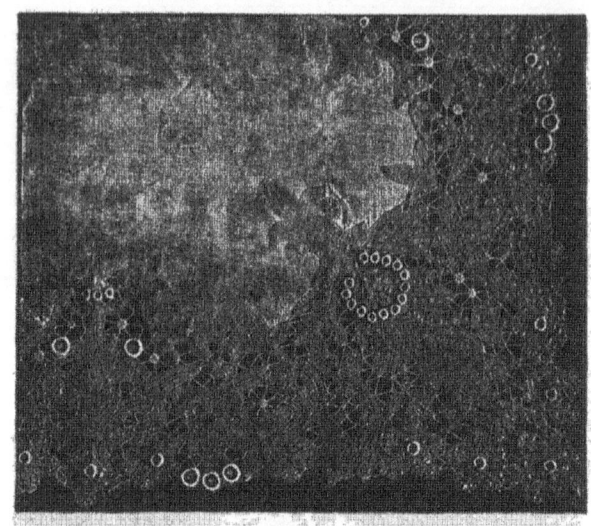

No. 65.—Design for Tea-Cloth Border and Corner in Battenburg Lace.

No. 66.—Point Lace Collar and Cuff.

No. 67.—Medallion in Point Lace.

5

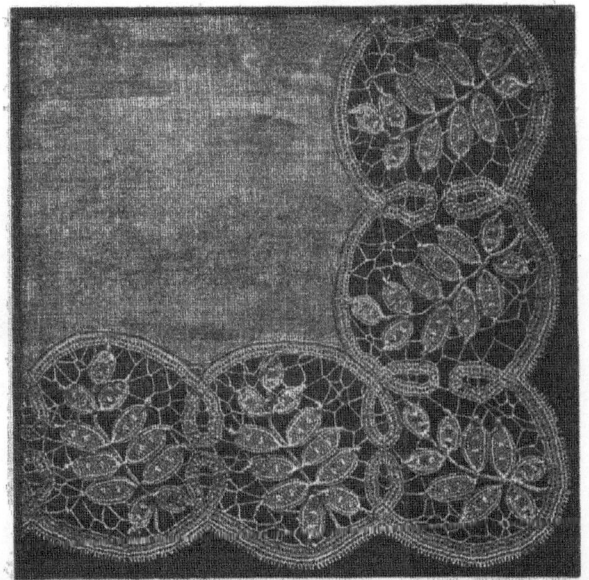

No. 68.—HANDKERCHIEF CORNER IN HONITON LACE.

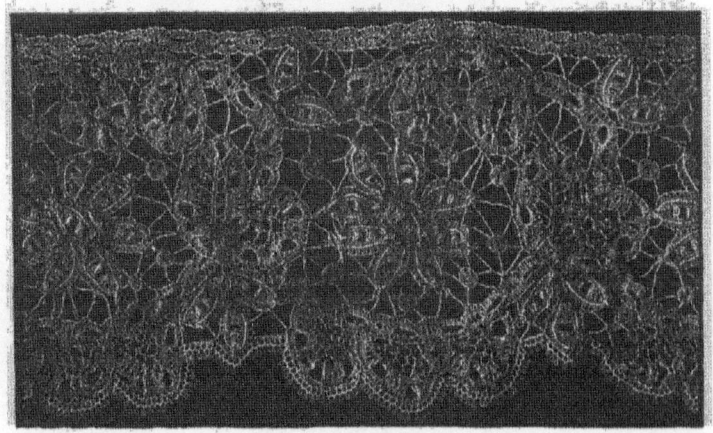

No. 69.—HONITON LACE EDGING.

No. 70.—HANDKERCHIEF IN PRINCESS LACE.

No. 71.—IDEAL HONITON FINGER-BOWL DOILY.

No. 72.—IDEAL HONITON FINGER-BOWL DOILY.

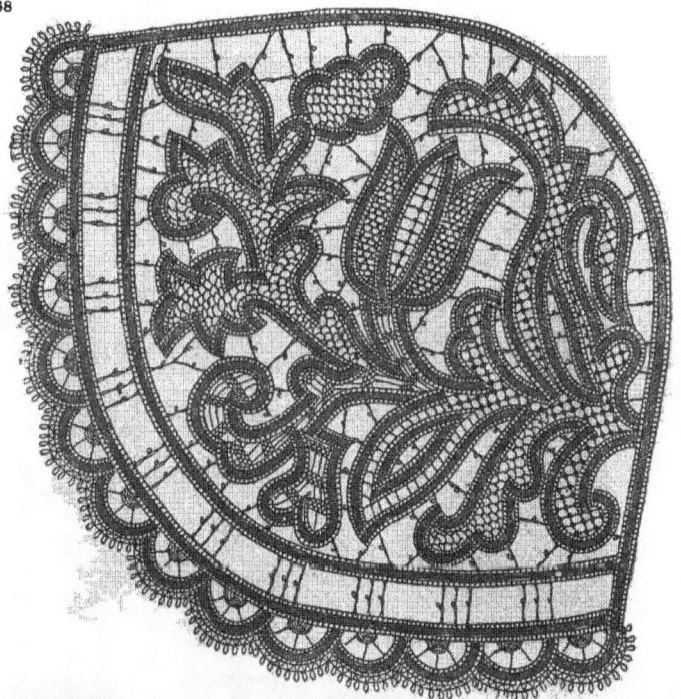

No. 73.—Side of Child's Cap in Battenburg Lace.

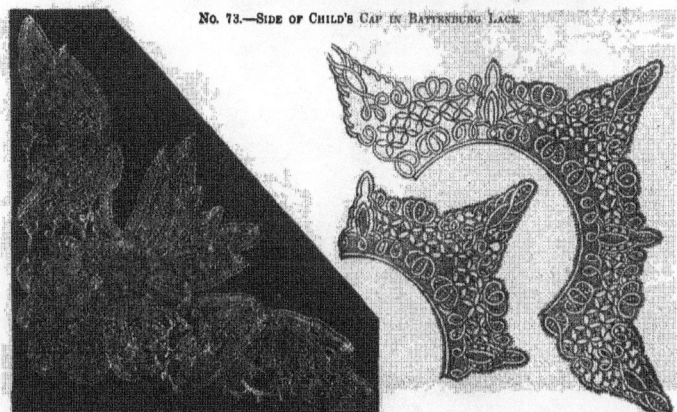

No. 74.—Corner of Battenburg
Lace for Napkin.

No. 75.—Collar and Cuff Design for
Princess Lace.

No. 76.—Center of Child's Cap in Battenburg Lace.

No. 77.—SQUARE IN IDEAL HONITON WORK.

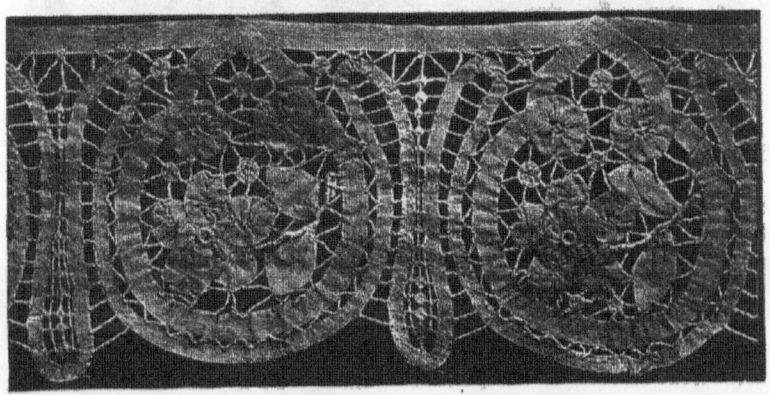

No. 78.—MODERN POINT DE BRUGES.

No. 79.—FLOUNCE IN BATTENBURG LACE (ONE-HALF THE ACTUAL WIDTH).

No. 80.—Honiton Lace Edging.

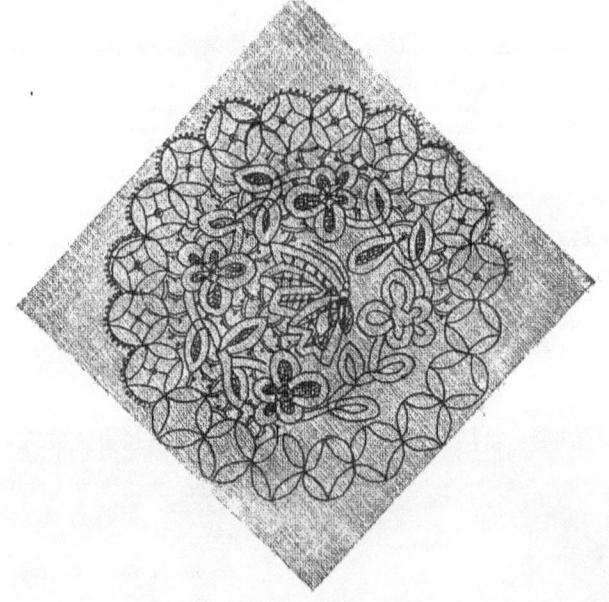

No. 81.—Princess Lace Doily Design.

No. 82.—DOILY IN NEEDLE-HONITON LACE.

No. 83.—ITALIAN LACE (HALF SIZE).

No. 84.—Tidy in Battenburg Lace.

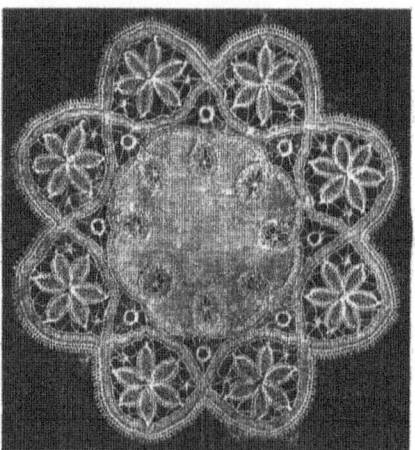

No. 85.—Point Lace Plate-Doily.

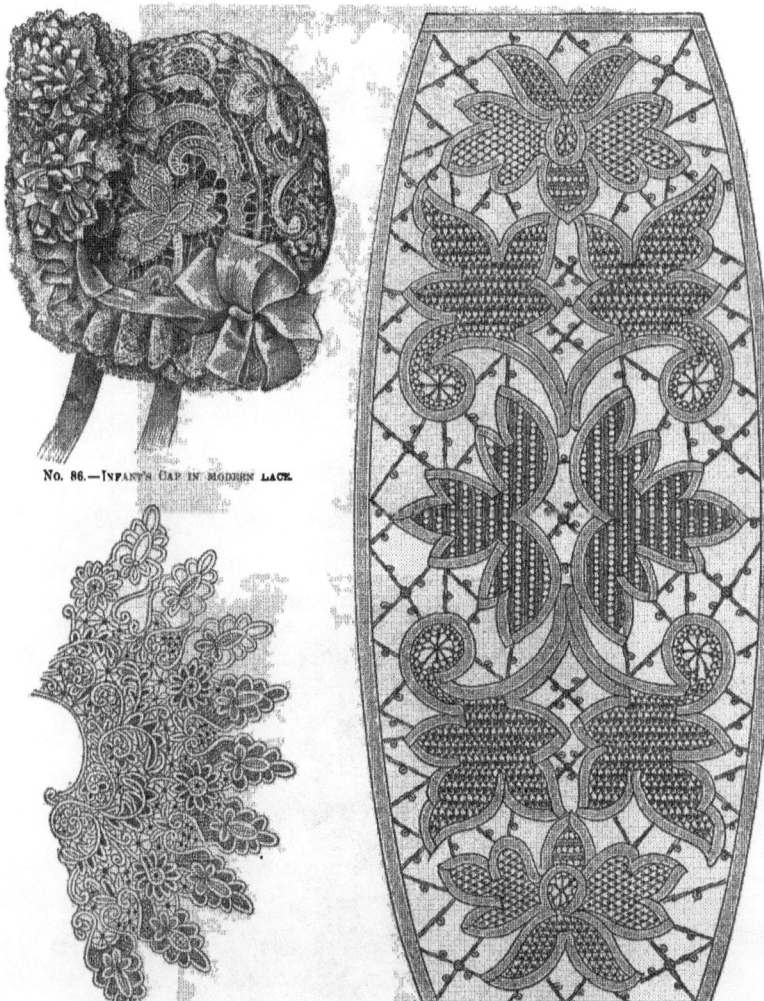

No. 86.—Infant's Cap in Modern Lace.

No. 87.—Design for Collar of Modern Lace.

No. 88.—Center of Infant's Cap in Modern Lace.

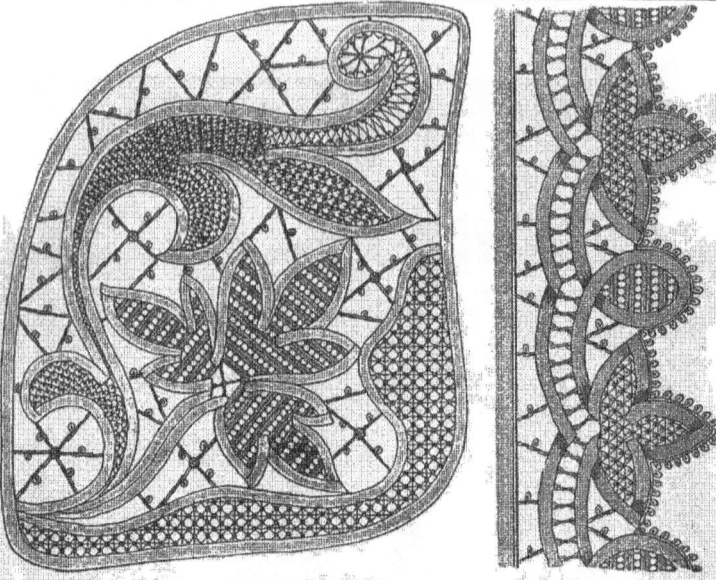

No. 89.—SIDE OF INFANT'S CAP IN MODERN LACE.

No. 90.—MODERN LACE EDGING.

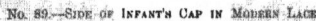

No. 91.—HANDKERCHIEF IN HONITON AND POINT LACE.

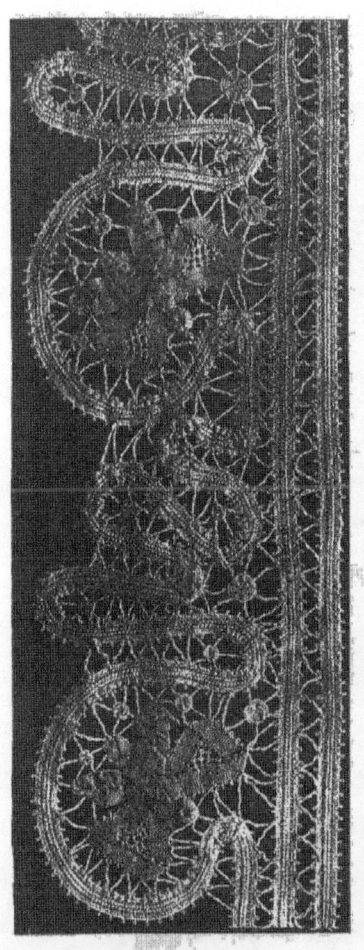

No. 92.—Bruges Lace Edging.   No. 93.—Sash-Curtain in Marie Antoinette Lace.

No. 95.—Design in Modern Lace.

No. 96.—Bureau-Scarf in Ideal Honiton Work.

No. 97.—Pillow Case for Baby Carriage (Ideal Honiton Work).

No. 98.—DOILY IN MODERN LACE.

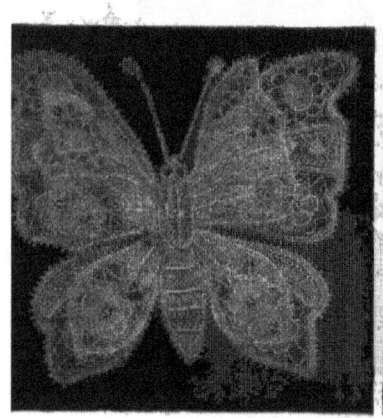

No. 99.—DOUBLE BUTTERFLY IN MODERN LACE.

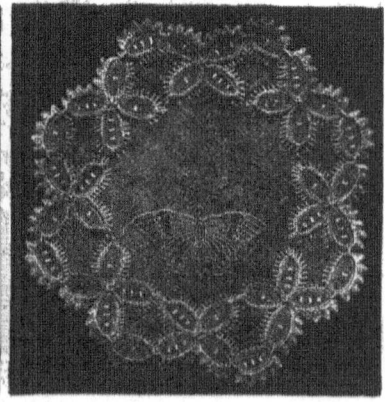

No. 100.—BUREAU-DOILY IN IDEAL HONITON WORK.

o

No. 101.—Table-Square in Battenburg Lace and Drawn-Work.

No. 103.—Design for
Straight Collar of
Battenburg Lace.

No. 102.—Design for Cuff of Battenburg Lace.

NOS. 104. AND 105.—FLARING COLLAR AND CUFF DESIGN FOR BATTENBURG LACE.

No. 106.—Ideal Honiton Doily for Olive-Tray.

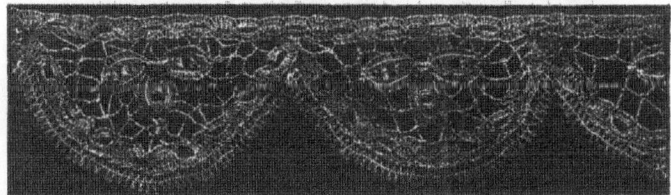

No. 107.—Honiton Lace Edging.

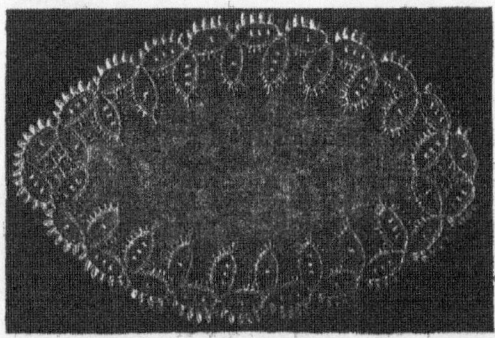

No. 108.—Ideal Honiton Doily for Salted-Almond Tray.

No. 109.—Table-Square of Linen with Renaissance Border.

No. 110.—Design in Honiton Lace.

No. 111.—IDEAL HONITON TABLE-SQUARE.

No. 112.—LIMOGES LACE EDGING.

No. 113.—POINT LACE DOILY FOR A TOILET CUSHION.

[No. 114.—SCARF END OF BATTENBURG LACE.

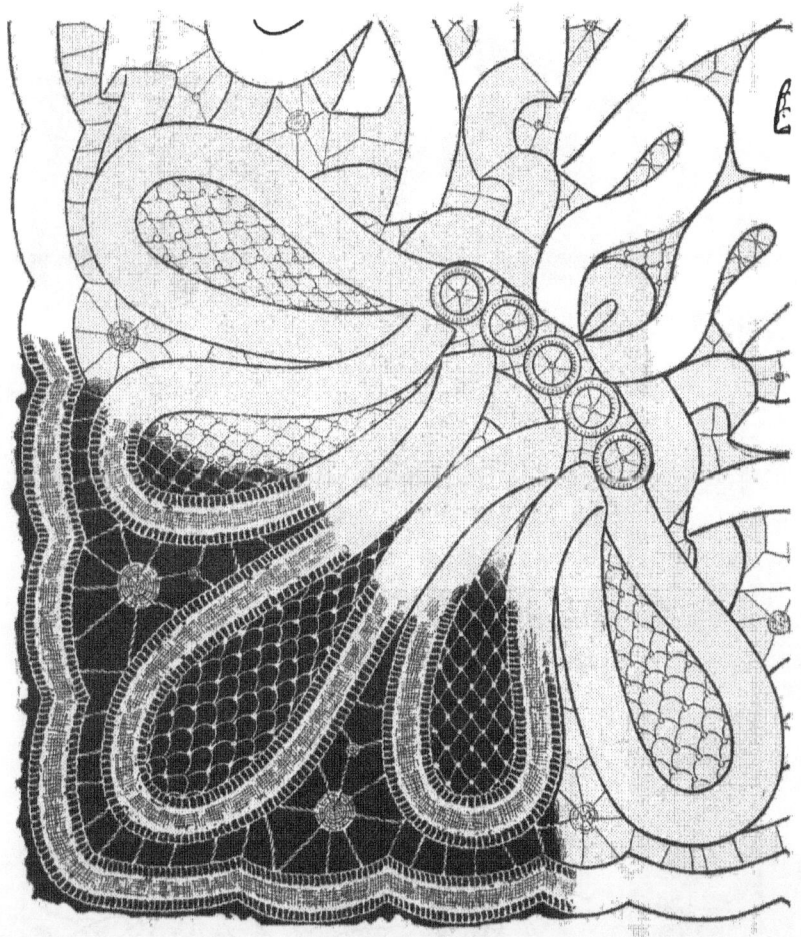

No. 115.—Corner of Portière Border in Battenburg Lace (In Full Size).

No. 116.- PORTIÈRE COMPLETED.

No. 118.—LACE BUTTERFLY.

No. 117.—DESIGN FOR INSERTION.

No. 119.—CORNER OF INSERTION FOR PORTIÈRE (REDUCED).

No. 121.—VENETIAN POINT LACE.

No. 120.—INSERTION FOR PORTIÈRE (REDUCED).   No. 122.—LACE BUTTERFLY.

No. 123.—MARIE ANTOINETTE CURTAIN-LACE.

No. 124.—Design for Fan in
Modern Lace.

NO. 126.—FAN IN MODERN LACE

NO. 125.—SAILOR COLLAR IN MODERN LACE.

No. 127.—Square of Marie Antoinette Lace.

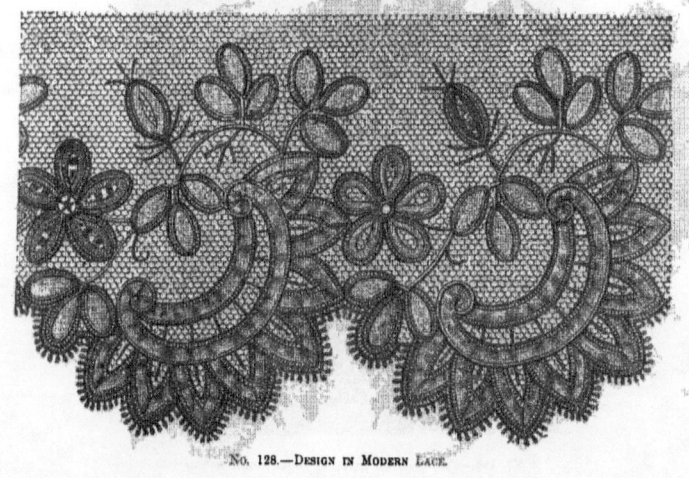

No. 128.—Design in Modern Lace.

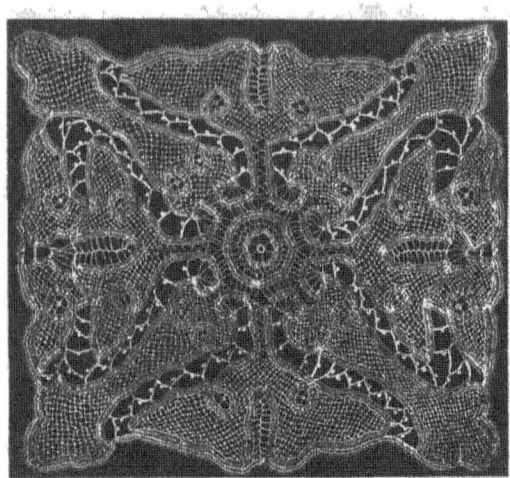

No. 129.—OBLONG DOILY OF POINT LACE.

No. 130.—FINGER-BOWL DOILY IN IDEAL HONITON WORK.

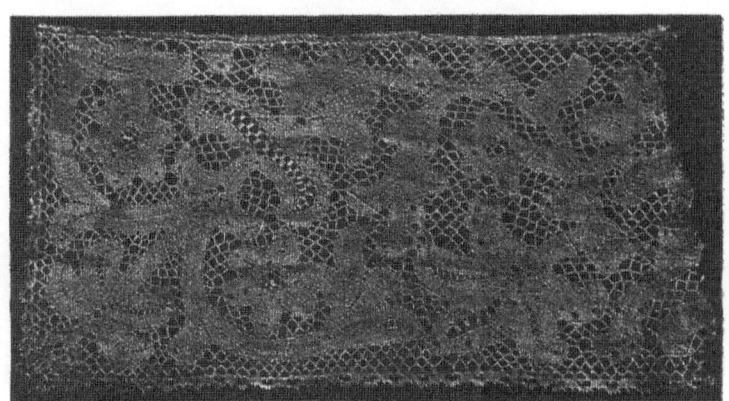

No. 131.—Design in Old Church Lace.

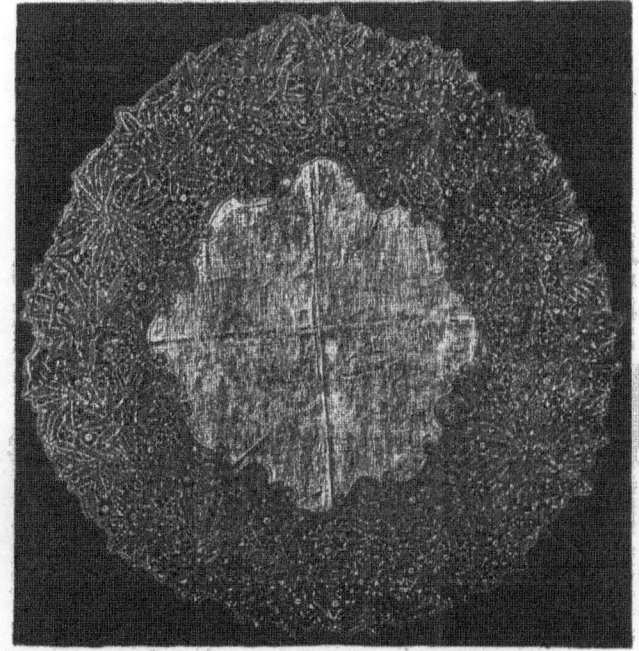

No. 132.—Circular Center-Piece of Linen with Needle-Point Border.

No. 133.—Royal Battenburg Lace Bureau-Scarf.

No. 134.—Tidy of Battenburg Lace.

7

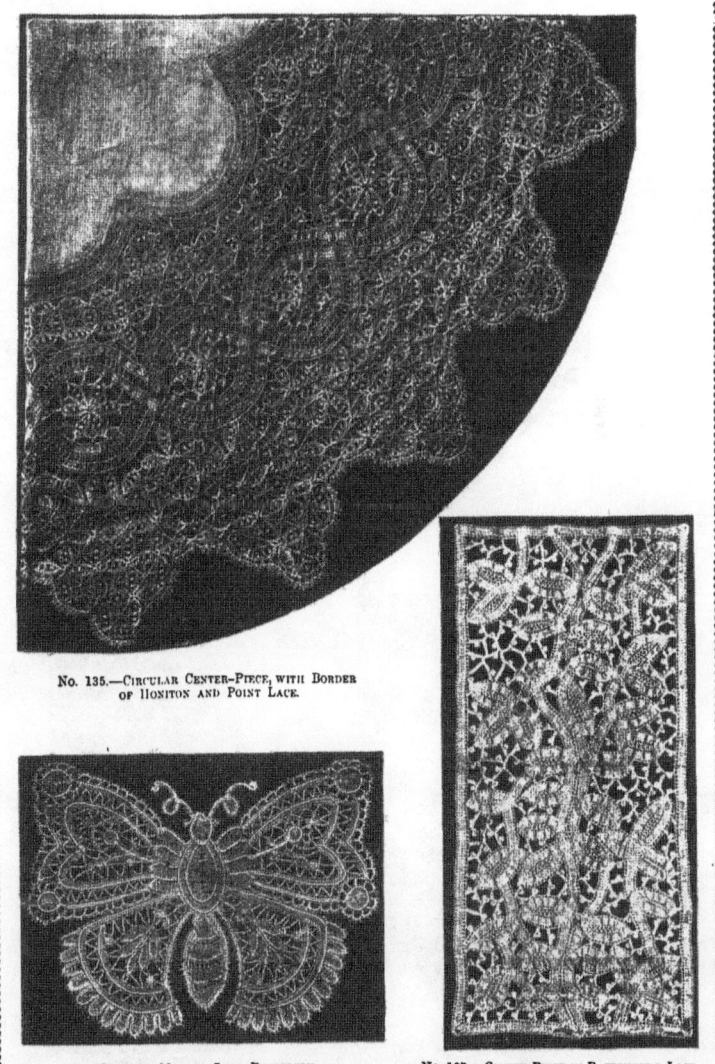

No. 135.—Circular Center-Piece, with Border
of Honiton and Point Lace.

No. 136.—Modern Lace Butterfly.   No. 137.—Center Piece in Battenburg Lace.

No. 138.—Plate-Doily to Match Circular Center-Piece on Page 98.

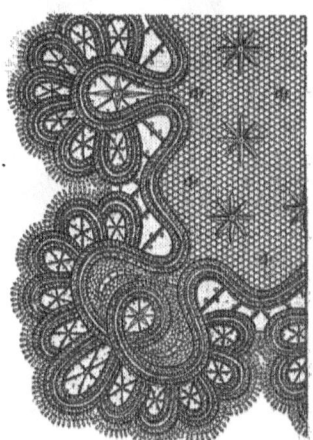

No. 139.—Tidy Border in Modern Lace.

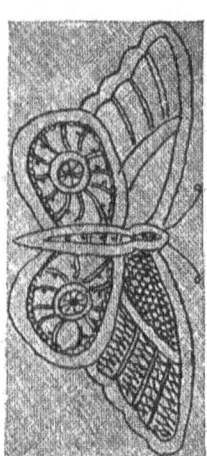

No. 140.—Design for a Butterfly in Point Lace.

No. 141.—BATTENBURG INSERTION, WITH CORD.

No. 143.—BATTENBURG LACE, WITH CORD.

No. 142.—BATTENBURG EDGING, WITH CORD.

No. 144.—BATTENBURG INSERTION, WITH CORD.

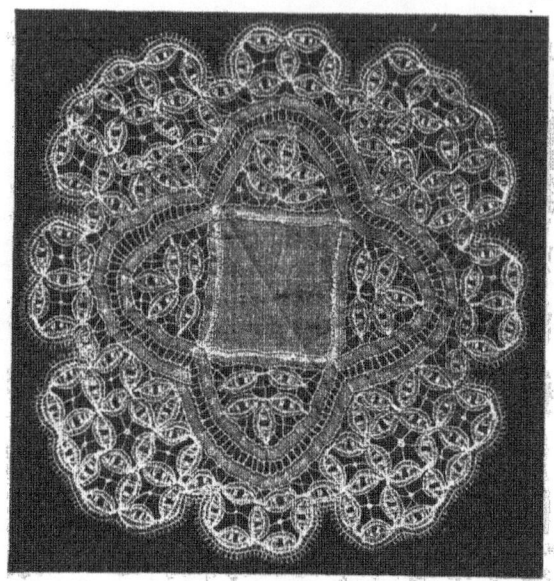

No. 145.—FINGER-BOWL DOILY IN PRINCESS LACE.

No. 146.—DESIGN FOR BATTENBURG EDGING.

No. 147. Tidy or Square of Needle-Point Lace.

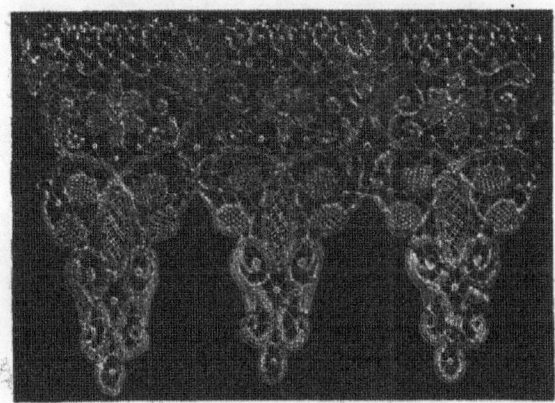

No. 148.—Point Lace (Actual Depth Ten Inches).

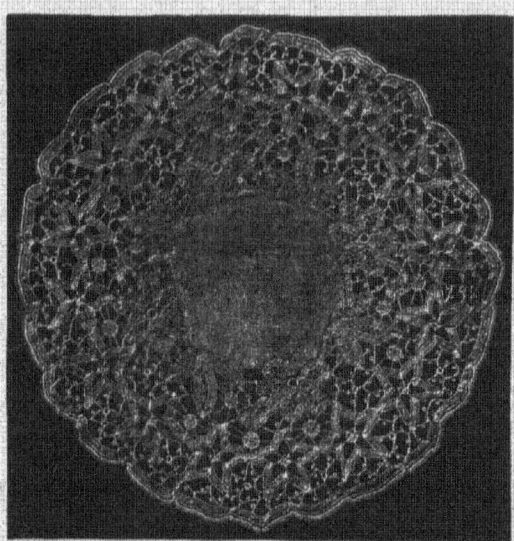

No. 149.—PLATE-DOILY OF LINEN LAWN AND NEEDLE-POINT LACE.

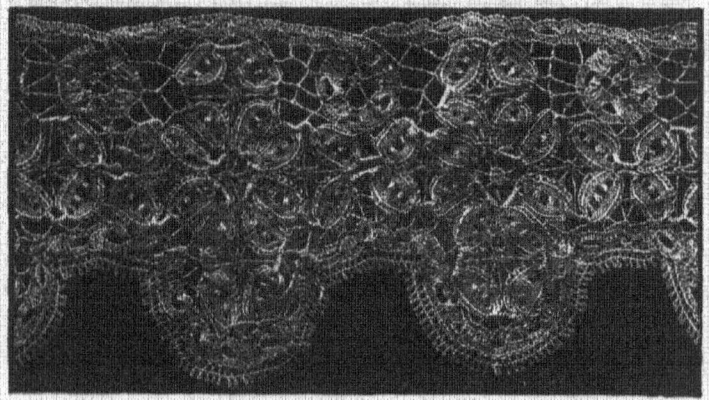

No. 150.—NEEDLE-POINT AND HONITON LACE EDGING.

No. 154.—Battenburg Church Lace.

No. 152.—ENGLISH NEEDLE-POINT.

No. 153.—HANDKERCHIEF   IN MODERN POINT LACE.

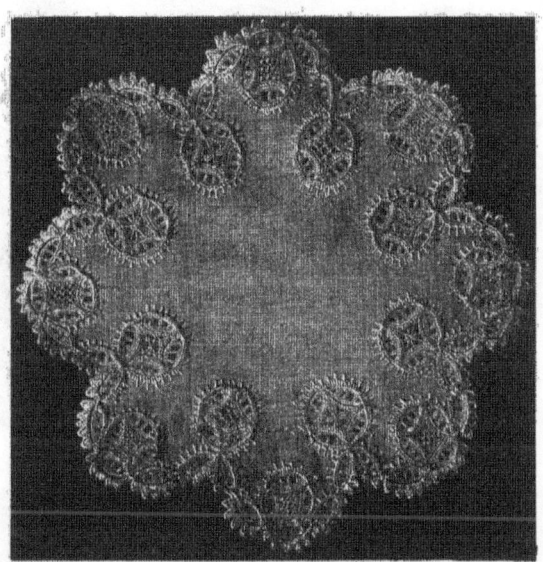

No. 154.—IDEAL HONITON BONBON DOILY.

No. 155.—DESIGN IN MODERN LACE.

No. 156.—Scarf-End in Modern Lace.

No. 157.—Modern Lace Edging.

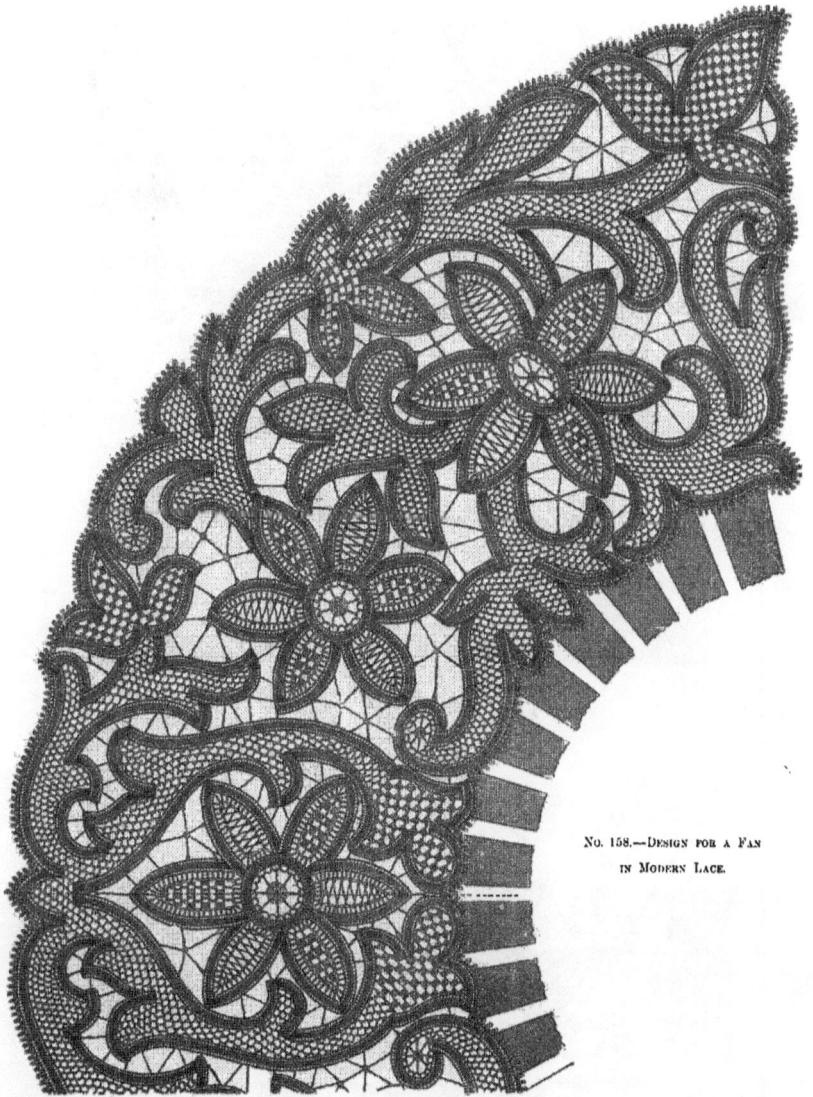

No. 158.—Design for a Fan
in Modern Lace.

No. 159.—Tea-Cloth in Royal Battenburg Lace.

Nos. 160 and 161.—Collar and Cuff Design (Battenburg and Honiton Laces).

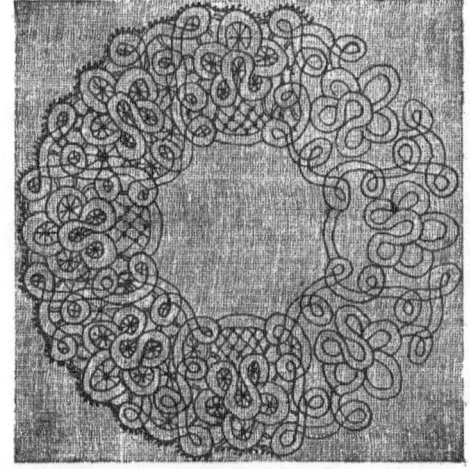

No. 162.—Design for a Doily or Handkerchief of Point or Honiton Lace. (Half Size.)

No. 164.—Design in Modern Lace.

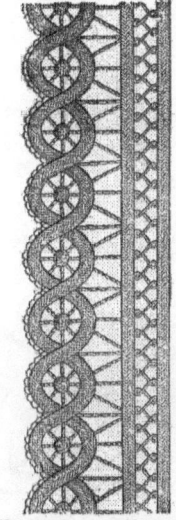

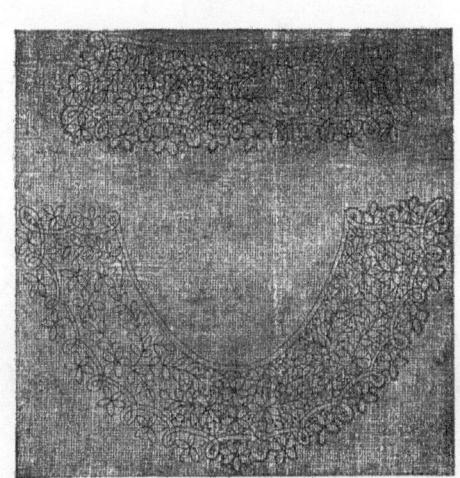

No. 163.—Design in Modern Lace.   No. 165.—Design for Princess or Duchesse Lace Collar and Cuffs.

No. 166.—DESIGN IN MODERN LACE.

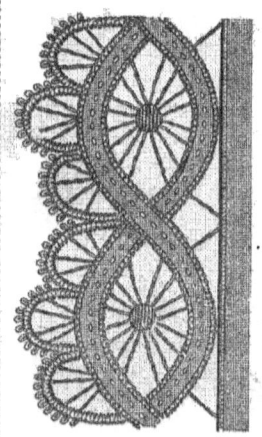

No. 167.—DESIGN IN MODERN LACE.   No. 168.—DESIGN FOR A CORNER IN BATTENBURG, POINT OR HONITON LACE.

No. 169.—Marie Antoinette Curtain Lace.

No. 170.—Ideal Honiton Finger-Bowl Doily.

No. 171.—Point Lace Finger-Bowl Doily.

No. 172.—TABLE-SQUARE IN HONITON LACE.

No. 173.—DESIGN IN MODERN LACE.

8

No. 174.—Corner of Handkerchief in Point Lace.

No. 175.—Battenburg or Point-Lace Collar and Cuff.

No. 176.—Rose-Bowl Square in Ideal Honiton Work.

No. 177.—Edging in Honiton and Point.

No. 178. — CORNER OF BATTEN-
BURG LACE, FOR SQUARES, ETC.

No. 180.—DOUBLE LACE BUTTERFLY.

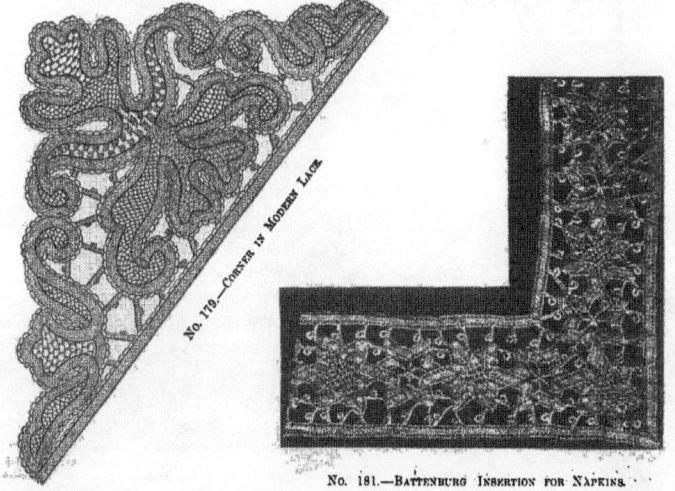

No. 179.—CORNER IN MODERN LACE.

No. 181.—BATTENBURG INSERTION FOR NAPKINS.

No. 182.—Square in Modern-Point Lace.

No. 183.—Design for a Butterfly in Point Lace. (Full Size.)

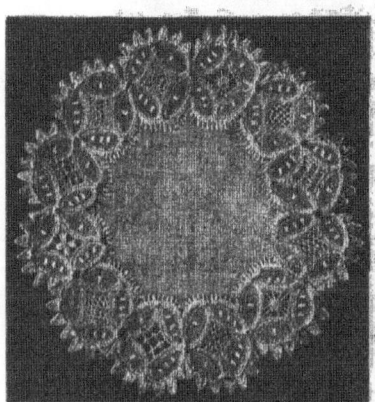

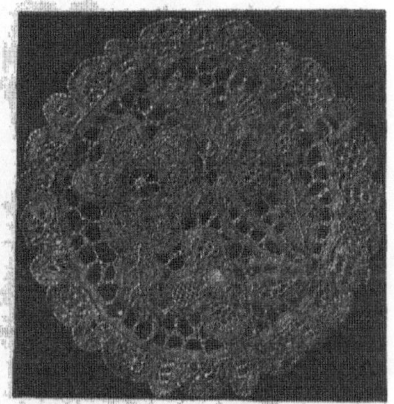

No. 184.—IDEAL HONITON FINGER-BOWL DOILY.　　　No. 185.—FINGER-BOWL DOILY OF POINT LACE.

No. 186.—DESIGN IN PRINCESS LACE.

No. 187.—CORNER OF HONITON LACE HANDKERCHIEF.

No. 188.—PUNCH-GLASS DOILY OF POINT LACE AND LAWN.

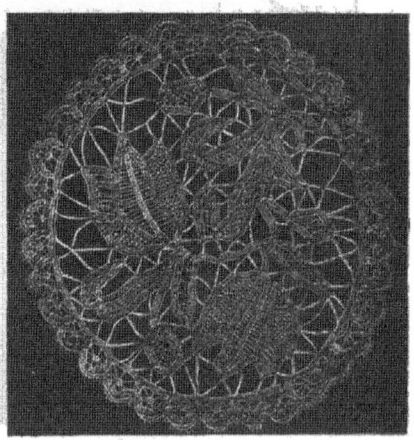

No. 189.—POINT LACE FINGER-BOWL DOILY.

No. 190.—ROYAL BATTENBURG BORDER FOR TABLE-SQUARE.

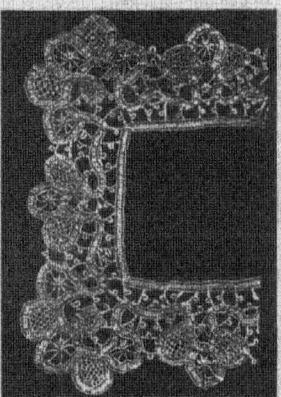

No. 191.—MODERN POINT LACE PUNCH-GLASS DOILY.

No. 192.—BATTENBURG BORDER FOR DOILEYS OR SQUARES.

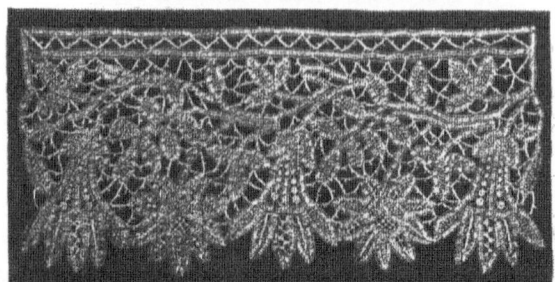

No. 193.—BATTENBURG LACE.

No. 194.—DOILY OF BATTENBURG LACE (FULL SIZE).

No. 195.—Pond Lily Design for Border to Center Piece
in Battenburg Lace.

No. 196.—Design for Modern Lace.

No. 197.—Design for Lace Cap for Elderly Ladies. (Modern Lace.)

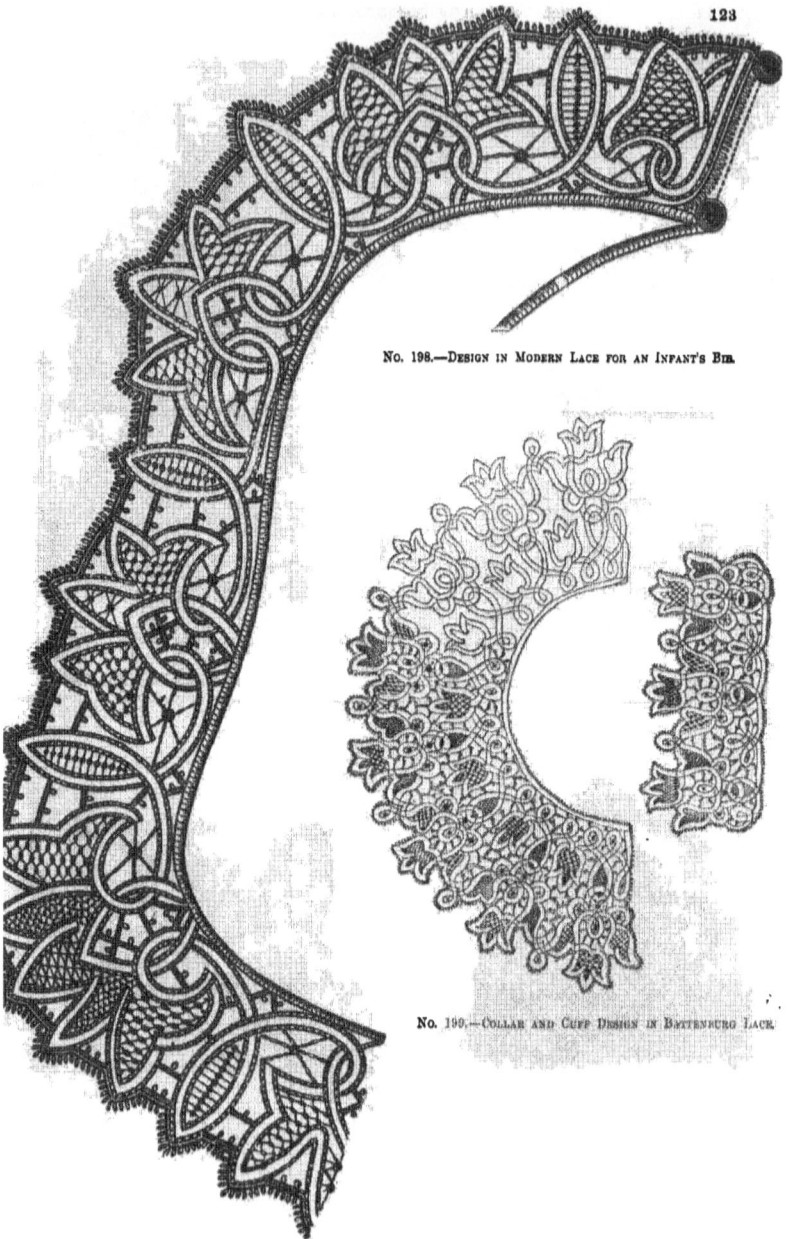

No. 198.—Design in Modern Lace for an Infant's Bib.

No. 199.—Collar and Cuff Design in Battenburg Lace.

No. 200.—Design for Tea-Cosey in Battenburg Lace.

3108

No. 201.—Tea-Cosey.   (Cut by Pattern No. 3108; one size; price 5d. or 10 cents.)

No. 202.—Butterfly Design for Point Lace.

No. 203.—RUSSIAN LACE.

No. 204.—APPLE DESIGN FOR A CORNER IN BATTENBURG LACE.

No. 205.—DESIGN FOR A HONITON LACE CAP.

No. 206.—Battenburg Insertion.

No. 207.—Battenburg Edging.

No. 208.—Royal Battenburg Lace.

No. 209.—Collar of Modern Lace.

No. 210.—Design in Modern Lace.

No. 211.—PILLOW-SHAM OF BATTENBURG LACE AND LINEN.

No. 212.—QUEEN ANNE TRAY-CLOTH OF BATTENBURG LACE AND LINEN.

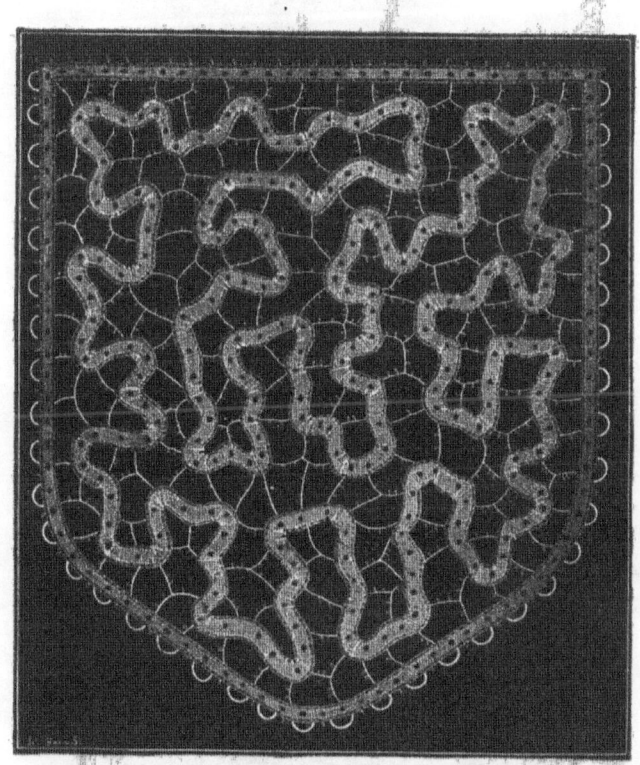

No. 213.—TAB OR SCARF-END IN ROMAN LACE (CORAL PATTERN).

No. 214.—Design for a Table-Scarf in Battenburg Lace.

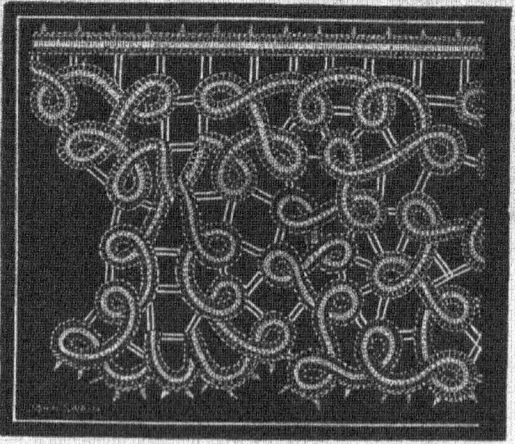

No. 215.—"Cardinal's Point" Lace.

No. 216.—Modern Russian Lace.

No. 217.—Corner in Modern Russian Lace.

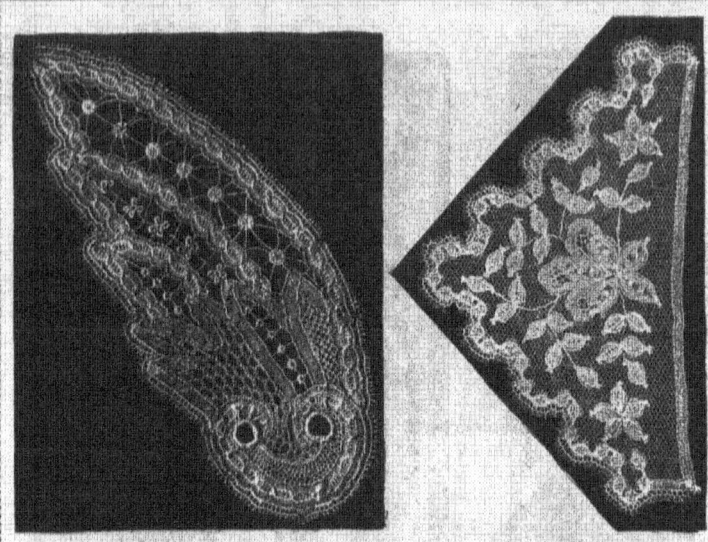

No. 218.—Wing in Modern Lace.   No. 219.—Cuff Point in Modern Appliqué.

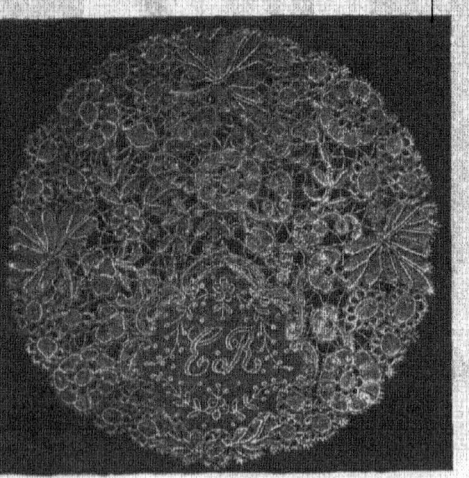

No. 220.—Point Lace Doily.

No. 221.   No. 222.   No. 223.

Nos. 221, 222 and 223.—Lace Bands for Stoles in Modern Lace.

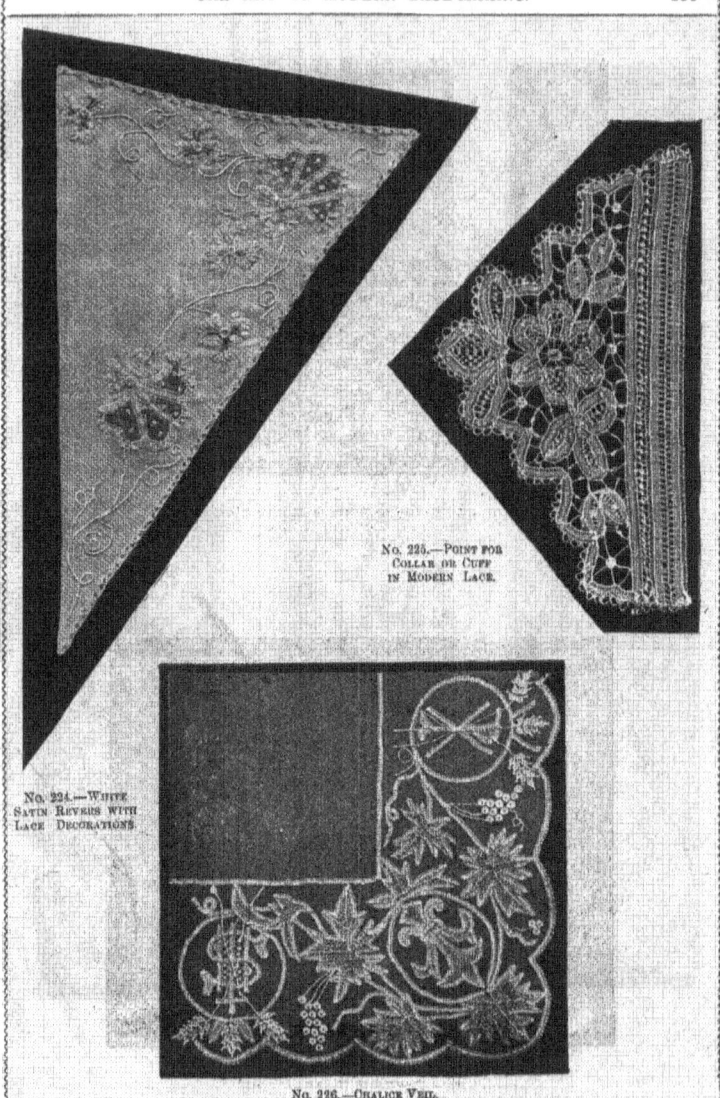

No. 225.—POINT FOR
COLLAR OR CUFF
IN MODERN LACE.

No. 224.—WHITE
SATIN REVERS WITH
LACE DECORATIONS.

No. 226.—CHALICE VEIL.

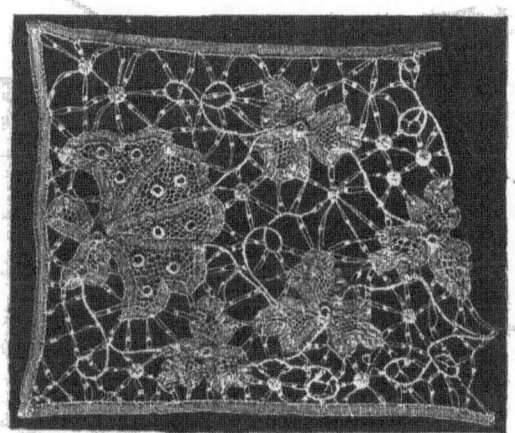

No. 227.—Section of Panel in Modern Lace.

No. 228.—Flounce in Modern Appliqué.

The Metropolitan Art Series.

THIS SERIES is published for the purpose of providing, in convenient form, practical lessons in those elegant and useful Arts, the cultivation of which is followed in the domestic circle. It will be devoted to all those nicer and daintier forms of occupation upon which many are pleased to expend their leisure hours.

Each Pamphlet of the Series will be complete in itself, forming a handbook of the particular art or employment upon which it will discourse. While the Explanations and Descriptions will be of the most careful and accurate character, there will be no dearth of illustration in any of the issues—in fact, the text of each volume will always be supplemented by engravings of the finest description.

The Metropolitan Art Series is issued Quarterly, for March, May, September and November.

The Subscription Price of the Series is 8s. or $2.00 per year.

The Price per Copy is 2s. or 50 Cents.

When two or more books of this series are ordered at one time from our London office, postage or carriage will be paid by us, but for single copies 3d. extra must be remitted to cover cost of sending.

Each Number is handsomely bound in fancy-colored, embossed paper, and presents an appearance as dainty as its contents are explicit and interesting.

ADDRESS:

THE BUTTERICK PUBLISHING CO. (LIMITED),

87 and 89, Paul Street, London, E. C., England;
or 7 to 17 West 13th Street, New York, U. S. A.